THE PERFECT COVER
FOR THE ULTIMATE EVIL

Remo knew what he had to do.

He had to go one-on-one against the foe that had left Chiun, the Master of Sinanju, a shadow of his former self, stripped of his most precious power.

He had to fight the force that had reduced icy, iron-willed Anna Chutesov to a quivering mass of fragile femininity and hot tears.

Remo had to battle the most awesome enemy he ever had to face.

A car wash.

A car wash?

The ideal disguise for the supreme engineer of dirty tricks. . . .

D1365462

"Warren Murphy and Molly Cochran have done it again. With *High Priest* they give their legions of readers a grand read as they tell the new adventures of the Grandmaster."
—Mary Higgins Clark, author of *Weep No More My Lady*

HIGH PRIEST

A Thriller by
Warren Murphy and Molly Cochran

The unforgettable characters of the national bestseller Grandmaster *return to the sudden-death game of global espionage. But the ruthless rivalry between these two enemies is dwarfed when a third player enters the contest—an opponent so powerful he makes murder seem like child's play. This riveting novel takes you on a compelling and hypnotic tour of the tense corridors of paranoia in Washington and Moscow and the deadly cold war forces that grip the world.*

The Destroyer

#72

SOLE SURVIVOR

Created by

WARREN MURPHY & RICHARD SAPIR

A SIGNET BOOK

NEW AMERICAN LIBRARY

PUBLISHER'S NOTE

This book is a work of fiction. Names, characters, places, and incidents either are the product of the author's imagination or are used fictitiously, and any resemblance to actual persons, living or dead, events, or locales is entirely coincidental.

SIGNET TRADEMARK REG. U.S. PAT. OFF. AND FOREIGN COUNTRIES
REGISTERED TRADEMARK—MARCA REGISTRADA
HECHO EN CHICAGO, U.S.A.

SIGNET, SIGNET CLASSIC, MENTOR, ONYX, PLUME, MERIDIAN and NAL BOOKS are published by NAL PENGUIN INC., 1633 Broadway, New York, New York 10019

First Printing, April, 1988

1 2 3 4 5 6 7 8 9

PRINTED IN THE UNITED STATES OF AMERICA

For Dave McDonnell and the gang at Starlog (Fangoria, too!)
And for technical adviser Spike MacPhee, Science-Fantasy Bookstore, Harvard Square, Third Planet from the Sun

The world was astounded when the first Soviet space shuttle blasted off into orbit.

Everyone knew that the Russians had been working on a shuttle of their own. But no one expected it to get off the ground. The Russians had finally licked the problem of cryogenic propulsion, but they couldn't come up with a reusable rocket motor. They tried to steal the secret from the French Ariane space program, but failed.

And so they resorted to the tactic that had enabled them to get Sputnik into orbit. They didn't build a better propulsion system, they built a bigger one. They mounted their main rocket engines onto the fat external fuel tank, strapped the shuttle to it, and augmented the system with four slender solid rocket boosters. The U.S. shuttle had used only two.

Once again, the Russians had solved a problem through brute force when patience and skill would have been more efficient.

In the Sputnik days, so long ago, they blew up rockets every third day until the law of averages ran in their favor and their tiny satellite achieved orbit. In the days of manned space flight, Russian cosmonauts lost their lives on the launching pad or in space, one for every five successful American man-in-space projects.

Thus, when the first Russian shuttle made it into space on the first try, the world was astonished.

"Amazing," said the President of the United States. "It didn't blow up."

"It isn't down yet, Mr. President," the Secretary of Defense replied. "They got it up there, but they haven't got it back in one piece. Not yet."

They were in the Situation Room in the White House basement. The walls were covered with giant computer simulation displays, which fed off a bank of manned consoles that received instantaneous data from orbiting satellites. The President had SINCNORAD on the line. The head of NORAD's Space Defense Operations Tracking Center was explaining over the phone link that the launch was half-expected.

"The Soviets have always operated this way," the general said. "Every time we announce something new, they break their necks to beat us to the punch. When we announced our first satellite program in the fifties, they sent up Sputnik. When we started shooting monkeys into orbit, they sent Gagarin up there. When we put our first man into space, they sent up the first woman. Now that we're about to resume our shuttle program, they do this to upstage us. Typical Russian thinking."

"But we beat them to the moon, right?" the President said. "We won that one."

"Yes, sir. Twenty years ago," the NORAD general said. "Times have changed. The Russians are beating the pants off of us in space."

"What is it doing up there?"

"Just orbiting so far," said the general. "But you can bet they're going to deploy a payload. The Soviets may be grandstanders, but they aren't doing this just for the show."

"I just want to know one thing," the President demanded. "Is their shuttle better than ours or not? I have to face the American people with this."

"It depends on how you look at it, sir."

"Look at it straight on, without blinking," the President said. "That usually works for me."

"Their new Energia booster system is clumsy. Too many boosters. Dangerous to launch. They should have waited. A few more years and they could have had reusable rocket motors attached to the shuttle itself. Instead, they have to jettison their motors when they ditch their external tank. Not cost-effective."

"It's a turkey, then?"

"Not exactly, sir. Their design is a carbon copy of ours. In place of the rocket motors, they've installed ordinary jet engines. They're smaller than rocket motors and that gives them a bigger payload bay. But the important thing is that the jet engines enable their shuttle to make a powered landing. It can land anywhere a 747 can. That's a major plus."

"I don't understand. Why doesn't our shuttle have that capability? We have jet engines too."

"Budget restrictions," answered the NORAD general.

"That I understand," said the President, who had just spent the morning arguing with the Speaker of the House over the mounting national debt. "Your intelligence sources are to be commended."

"Thank you, Mr. President," said the general, neglecting to mention that he'd gotten everything out of his office file of *Aviation Week*.

The President replaced the phone. Over the loudspeaker system of the Situation Room, the intercepted communications from the Soviet shuttle crew were reproduced. Listening to the two-way chatter, the President wished he knew conversational Russian. An NSA stenographer was rapidly transcribing the communications into translated English on a shorthand machine. The President looked at the unreeling strip of paper blankly. He didn't read shorthand either.

"They're up to something up there," the President told the Secretary of Defense grimly.

"They're also in trouble," the Secretary of Defense, who did know shorthand, said suddenly.

At first Mission Commander Alexei Petrov did not think the spinning object was a threat.

He sat at the controls of the first Soviet space shuttle, commissioned the *Yuri Gagarin* in honor of the first man in space, and watched the metallic object through the big vacuum-insulated cabin windows.

The object appeared to be a meteorite on a collision course with earth. It was small and misshapen, not much larger than a toaster. Commander Petrov was not concerned about the possibility of colliding with the meteorite. In the vastness of space, meteorites were no more a threat than they were on earth. A hit was possible, but the odds of such a freak accident happening were about the same as being struck by lightning during a rainstorm.

Commander Petrov's attention was drawn to the object because it moved more slowly than a meteorite being drawn into the earth's gravitational field should. Much too slowly.

"Look there," he told his copilot, cosmonaut Oleg Gleb.

Gleb followed Petrov's pointing finger. "I see it," he said excitedly. Gleb was the mission's exobiologist, which meant that he was schooled in the subject of life beyond the earth. Inasmuch as life beyond the earth had not so far been discovered, Gleb's specialty was only a little more practical than psychiatry. "But what is it?" he asked.

"I do not know," answered Petrov, "but it now appears to be spinning in our direction."

"Yes. I agree. It has changed direction toward us. What do we do?"

"Request orders."

"But it will be upon us before the chain of command can issue an informed decision."

"Then my hand will accidentally trip the maneuvering thrusters while you communicate with Star City."

Suiting action to words, Commander Alexei Petrov pressed the control yoke with both hands. Thruster jets sent the shuttle tipping away from the approaching object, which resembled a clump of fused nickels.

"*Yuri Gagarin* to Cosmograd. Acknowledge please, Star City," said Cosmonaut Gleb as he watched, with widening eyes, the strange spinning object appear to change course again. "We have an unidentified object closing on us. Orders, please."

"Describe object," demanded ground control.

"Not a satellite, not a meteor, not otherwise identifiable," sputtered Cosmonaut Gleb as the object reversed its spinning motion as if locking in on them. It continued to close.

"Be more specific," said ground control in that infuriatingly steady monotone. Don't those fools realize that we might possibly be under attack? thought Gleb.

Mission Commander Alexei Petrov jumped into the conversation.

"I am taking evasive action, but the object continues to follow us. What do we do?"

"Do not take evasive action without orders," Cosmograd insisted. Then the voice went away, obviously to confer with higher authorities. In Russia, there were always higher authorities and no one courageous enough to make a decision in a crunch.

"*Chert vozmi!*" Petrov swore harshly. "Do they not care about us? What about our mission?"

Faster than either cosmonaut expected, an answer crackled uplink. It was two words. Brittle and inexplicable.

"Attempt salvage."

"Repeat," said Petrov.

"Attempt to capture this foreign object in your cargo doors."

"What about our payload? The satellite may be damaged."

"We can always build another satellite. Attempt salvage."

Cosmonauts Alexei Petrov and Oleg Gleb exchanged sick glances, but there was no time to think. The spinning object was closer now, its pitted surface more clearly discernible.

Petrov threw the yoke to bring the *Yuri Gagarin* about while Gleb got on the intership radio and alerted the third crewman, Engineer Igor Ivanovitch, to don his spacesuit and prepare to retrieve an object from the cargo bay.

"Do you not mean 'deploy'?" asked Ivanovitch. "You have not deployed while I slept, have you?"

"Just get into the suit," Gleb barked as Petrov sent the shuttle soundlessly tipping so that its cargo doors faced the sun and the approaching object. Petrov threw the great lever that sent the massive cargo bay doors on the top of the shuttle yawning wide like a white beetle spreading its wings. And then he shut his eyes tightly. It was out of his hands now.

When several minutes passed without the sound of an impact, he knew that the object was not one of the feared Star Wars devices of the American National Space Administration. He knew all about those. Satellite killers were being developed at a furious pace by America's Hollywood President and named after a war-mongering Hollywood movie. At least that was how the party commentators described it on the *Bremya* TV news program. Because he was a privileged cosmonaut, Petrov managed to locate a bootlegged videotape of the *Star Wars* film. Even though it was a twelfth-generation print and as full of snow as a Moscovite's boots, Petrov thought it was more exciting than all of Russia's TV shows put together. If too violent.

When ten minutes passed, Petrov broke the silence.

"We are still breathing," he told Cosmonaut Gleb.

"The ship is undamaged," Gleb agreed. Neither man mentioned the fact that their training had required donning spacesuits at this critical time. Both understood it would be better to die instantly from the explosively cold vacuum of space than to die slowly in the limited-oxygen environment of a suit, radioing their last observations for the benefit of the bloodless scientists at Cosmograd, nicknamed Star City by the Americans.

Petrov got on the intership link. "Comrade Ivanovitch, I am now closing the cargo bay doors. You will enter the cargo bay and report on what you find there."

"What should I expect to find there?" Ivanovitch asked in a sleepy but nervous voice.

"You will tell me, and not I you. Keep your suit radio link open."

"*Da*, Comrade Commander," said Ivanovitch. To himself he muttered the choice Russian phrase "*Po zhopu*," meaning, "Up yours."

Petrov and Gleb listened pensively as the sounds of Ivanovitch's measured breathing came over the intership system.

"I am opening the first airlock," said Ivanovitch.

Indicator lights on the control panel confirmed that the airlock door had opened.

"I am closing the first airlock door," said Ivanovitch. "I am in the airlock now."

"He is very brave," whispered Gleb.

"He is third in command," said Petrov. "If he fails, it
will be your responsibility next."

"Now I am opening the second airlock door," said
Ivanovitch. "I can now see into the cargo bay."

"What do you see?" demanded Petrov. "Describe it,
please."

"I see the satellite, still in its net, ready for deployment."

"Look for something smaller, like a meteor."

"I am entering the cargo bay," said Ivanovitch.

Suddenly the *Yuri Gagarin* shuddered. The yoke in
Petrov's hand vibrated like a living thing. He gripped it
with both hands, thinking wildly that they were doomed.

The control panel went crazy. Lights blinked and
flashed, and levers swung of their own accord. The *Yuri
Gagarin*, its retros firing spasmodically, turned slow
pirouettes in the void of orbital space.

"We are haunted!" screeched Gleb.

"Shut up!" snapped Petrov, who did not believe in
ghosts. But memories of another grainy American videotape, one called *Aliens*, flashed into his mind, and he
hastily plugged himself into a relief tube before he
released his bladder all over the high-traction flooring.

When he was done, Commander Petrov tried to raise
Ivanovitch.

"Ivanovitch! Ivanovitch! Are you safe?"

There was no answer.

"He will answer," Gleb said frantically, knowing that
if Ivanovitch did not, he himself would be ordered into
the cargo bay next. "Give him time."

But five minutes of repeated entreaties for Ivanovitch
to answer brought only static.

"You know your duty," Alexei Petrov told Oleg Gleb
meaningfully.

"*Da*," said Gleb weakly. He shook Petrov's cold hand
stiffly, as if in farewell, and slipped down the winding

aluminum stair to the lower deck where the spacesuits were racked.

"I am opening the first airlock," Gleb's voice came back moments later. "I am now in the cargo bay. The lights are on."

"Do you see Ivanovitch?"

"No," said Gleb in a voice so low-pitched it might have come from a dead man.

"Look harder," said Petrov. "He must be there somewhere."

"I see only the satellite," Gleb answered, anguished.

"Never mind," said Commander Alexei Petrov in a sick voice. "I know where Ivanovitch is."

"You do?"

"*Da*, he is outside the ship, floating not ten feet in front of my face."

"I do not remember you opening the cargo bay doors after Ivanovitch entered," Gleb pointed out.

"I did not. They must have opened during the malfunction."

"Then I may leave this place now?"

"No. Look for the object," said Petrov, repressing a shudder as silver-flecked pieces of Ivanovitch's pressure suit drifted away. No doubt the rest of the late Igor Ivanovitch was now spinning through empty space.

"I am looking for the object now," said Gleb.

"It may have floated out with Ivanovitch."

"No!" said Gleb excitedly. "I see it! I see it!"

"Describe it!"

"It is exactly as it appeared when first sighted. A pitted clump of metal. One side is smooth, as if machined. It has attached itself to the cargo bay doors manual control board."

"Magnetic?"

"It must be so."

"Attempt to remove it."

"I am doing that now," Gleb said, exertion twisting his voice. "But it will not disengage."

"No magnet could be that powerful, could it?" demanded Petrov.

"Commander," Gleb said wonderingly, "it does not appear to be merely attached to the control board. It appears to have fused itself to the board."

"Fused?"

"The edges of the board where it touches this object have grown out into the object. This is most passing strange."

"It is more than passing strange," said Commander Petrov.

"What do I do?"

"Let me think."

Commander Alexei Petrov stared out the windows into the star-sprinkled deeps of space. Faraway now, he recognized a luminous shape like a deformed silver starfish as the mangled remains of Cosmonaut Ivanovitch. He quickly flipped the switch that reestablished a voice downlink to Cosmograd. To his surprise, there was no uplink. He checked his telemetry indicators. The downlink was dead too. He was cut off from all communications with earth.

Alexei Petrov switched to the intership communicator.

"We have lost ground communications," he informed his copilot in a voice more steady than he felt.

"This . . . this thing must be the cause," Gleb called back. "It is affecting our electronics. It must have caused that earlier malfunction."

"Await me, Gleb. I am coming with tools. We must remove that leech of a thing from our electronics."

"Hurry," said Oleg Gleb.

Commander Alexei Petrov scrambled into his pressure suit, twisted the helmet on its ring mounting, and drank in the sterile-tasting oxygen/nitrogen mixture. It lifted his heart, which was racing more rapidly now. Toolbox under one arm, he made his way clumsily to the airlock. The outer door was open. Strange. Gleb should have closed it behind him.

Commander Petrov poked his head into the cargo bay. He saw the satellite, whose purpose was unknown to him, still cradled in a restraining net of nylon filaments, like a mirrored ball in a spider's web. He saw also the shiny lumpish thing which clung to the control board like a half-melted ice cube.

But he did not see Oleg Gleb.

Perhaps Oleg was behind the satellite, just outside the range of his own vision. Yes, that must be it, Petrov told himself. Oleg is behind the satellite.

But a slight doubt flickered through Petrov's mind. He smelled, within the confines of his suit, a sudden rush of odor. A stale, sweaty odor. His visor began to steam. Petrov swore at his own infantile reaction to fear. There was nothing to be frightened of within the cargo bay. Just an unusual technical problem caused by a peculiar meteorite which must be magnetic because it had followed the shuttle through evasive maneuvers. Yes, that was it. The meteor was magnetic. That would explain everything—why it stuck to the control board and its strange effect on the *Yuri Gagarin's* complicated electronics.

But still Alexei Petrov could not will his booted feet to step over the threshold of the airlock.

He touched his throat mike to cover his indecision.

"Oleg. I am here."

No answer.

"Oleg?" His voice was tighter now. Surely Oleg was behind the satellite. Oleg was playing a joke. Yes, that was it. A joke to relieve the tension.

Alexei Petrov laughed nervously.

"Very funny, Oleg. But enough. Show yourself. I

have brought tools, and they are very heavy. Come help me." He added that last part because, like a child at the door of a supposedly haunted house, he was not going to enter the cargo bay alone. Oleg would have to show himself first, show that it was indeed safe to enter.

But Oleg did not show himself.

Finally Alexei Petrov steeled himself to cross the threshold. His boot bumped something on the floor.

Commander Petrov looked down. It was then that he saw the liquid coating on the floor—the red liquid coating. There was no time for his conscious mind to register the meaning of that coating before he saw the object his boot had stubbed.

It was impossible to bend over in a spacesuit, but if one slowly scrunched down, one could lower his body into a half-crouch. Alexei Petrov did so, the hissing of his oxygen tanks filling his ears.

The object was a cube of varicolored material streaked with metallic silver, like the outer surface of his own cosmonaut suit. Carefully Petrov picked it up in his gloved hand. It was much, much heavier than it should have been. It was only slightly bigger than a child's building block.

Coming to his feet, Petrov held the cube up to his visor. He wiped at the visor to clear the condensation that obscured his vision. But of course it was his breath causing the misting, and it was no more possible to wipe the inside of the visor than it was to scratch his itchy nose.

The cube dripped. The liquid was red, like blood. But it was too pale for blood, too thin. It could not be blood, Petrov told himself. Yet the cube was spongy to his touch, like an organ. Petrov squeezed it and felt it give, but under the surface, his fingers encountered hardness.

On one side of the cube there was a peculiar indentation. As if a nut-and-bold assembly had been pressed into the cube. There were even the impressions of the bolt threads lining the indentation. Just like the bolts of the inner airlock's walls. The same size, too. Petrov experimentally pressed the cube to one of the protruding bolts. A perfect fit. Too perfect. Abruptly Alexei Petrov decided the cube bore further examination. In the safety of the control room. Oleg could wait.

Petrov went to the airlock door. But it refused to respond to the electronic controls. He tried manual. And as he tugged on the frozen lever, it became dark.

Alexei Petrov could not hear the closing of the airlock door leading to the cargo bay—not while sealed in a pressure suit with that damned oxygen hissing in his ears. But when he turned, he saw that he was locked into the airlock.

Oleg again.

"This is not humorous, Oleg," Alexei Petrov shouted into his helmet mike. "I order you to open the airlock and show yourself. Do you hear me, Oleg? Cosmonaut Gleb, your superior has given you a direct order. You will obey this at once. At once, do you hear?"

But Cosmonaut Oleg Gleb still did not answer.

"Damn!" Alexei Petrov swore. He threw the cube of unidentifiable matter at the stubborn airlock door. It bounced back like a rubber ball. Reflexively he caught it. A piece of the silver streaking came off, revealing something familiar embedded in the whitish surface beneath. It was writing. No, not writing, Petrov saw as he looked closer. Embroidery. Very, very tiny embroidery. The stitching spelled out a single word: Gleb.

Commander Alexei Petrov threw up. A splash of vomit coated the inside of his visor and ran hotly down his chest. He tried to wipe it away, but of course he could not.

Petrov grabbed for the airlock controls, the ones leading into the cargo bay. He did not wish to go into the cargo bay, but he did not fear that as much as he feared to remain in the airlock. He frantically punched the buttons, but the door refused to open. It was frozen.

Sobbing, unable to see clearly past the yellowish film of vomit coating his visor, Petrov fought the manual controls. They were stuck. He licked at the inside of his visor to clear it, spitting the acid taste down his suit.

Then the walls began to move.

Commander Alexei Petrov felt the strength go from his legs. He did not fight. He did not cry or scream or even pray. He was beyond those things. He slid to the slick red floor next to the soft cube, and because he thought he understood what the cube had been, he looked for a second cube. He saw it sitting in a corner, and then he knew for certain how he would die.

Alexei Petrov watched the walls closing in on him, the exposed bolts seeking to press into his too-soft flesh.

His last thought was to wonder how it was possible. He had helped build the *Yuri Gagarin* and there was no mechanism that would enable the airlock walls to contract like that. It was simply not possible for the Soviet shuttle to demonstrate the characteristics of an American trash compactor.

In the Situation Room of the White House, the President listened to the Secretary of Defense's rapid-fire translations of the shorthand transcript of Star City's frantic demands that the *Yuri Gagarin* acknowledge transmission.

"They just repeat the same message over and over," the Secretary of Defense said. "But the shuttle is silent."

"Malfunction?" wondered the President.

"I doubt it. I think it may have something to do with

the object the crew claimed they encountered. There's a distinct possibility, Mr. President, that the craft and crew are casualties."

The President nodded. It was regrettable, tragic. But at least it was a Soviet craft this time. Perhaps now the American public would fully understand the dangers of space exploration.

In the background, the Russian calls for the *Yuri Gagarin* to respond repeated endlessly, the voice of the mission supervisor sinking into a weary monotone.

Then suddenly there came an answer. A voice that was flat, metallic, and entirely without accent or inflection. And the voice spoke in English. It said:

"Hello is all right."

2

His name was Remo and all he wanted to do was help the homeless.

Below, Washington D.C. was a blaze of light, its white buildings pristine and ethereal. It was a city designed to be beautiful. By night it was. Artistically arranged spotlights made the Capitol resemble a temple of the ancient world. The White House was a shrine. The Lincoln Memorial was a fragment of the Greek Empire.

By day, it had appeared different. The buildings were grimy; the city beyond the fringes of the seat of government for the most powerful nation on earth was a ghetto. But by night it breathed the high ideals on which it had been built.

Remo spanked pollution particles off his palms. He had picked up the grit climbing the cold obelisk that was the Washington Monument. Normal people did not get their hands dirty climbing the Washington Monument. But then, normal people took the indoor stairs during normal visiting hours. Remo Williams had climbed the north face of the marble needle with his bare hands.

He was a young-looking man in simple clothes—tan chinos and a black T-shirt. His eyes were brown, his hair was a darker brown, and his unblemished skin held a light tan which even the ground spotlights could not whiten. He looked normal. In fact, he looked average.

His one distinguishing feature was a pair of abnormally thick wrists which he rotated absently.

With eyes that were more than normal, he scanned the city for the teeming legions of homeless and displaced persons that the TV anchorman had said, in doleful tones, were so numerous in America that they swarmed in the cradle of Liberty itself. He called it America's shame.

Remo, who had been born in America and raised as an orphan wanted to see all these homeless people for himself. He wanted to help. That was all. It would be one of his final services for the land that nurtured him, before he left it for good.

The trouble was, he couldn't find any homeless in the streets of Washington, D.C. Not during the day. And not again at night, when the nip of early spring dwindled into the chill of late winter. The homeless would show themselves at night, Remo thought. They would come out to sleep on the steamy grates of the Washington subway or crawl into cardboard boxes just off Massachusetts Avenue.

But wandering the streets, Remo had found no homeless people. Just the ordinary citizens of an inner city— the winos, the drug addicts, the petty street crooks, and the other kind—who wore three-piece suits and held forth in law offices and corporate boardrooms.

As a last resort, Remo had climbed the Washington Monument, knowing that if there were any homeless prowling the streets below, his abnormally keen eyes would spot them from that high perch.

Finally Remo did see someone. An old woman pushing a shopping cart filled to overflowing with plastic bags stuffed with dirty clothes and old newspapers.

Remo pushed himself off the blunt top of the Washington Monument and twisted in midair so that he clamped the north and east faces of the obelisk with his body. Applying intermittent pressure with the toes of his Italian loafers and using the clamping force of his arms to maintain his vertical position, he slid down the monument like a spider slipping down his web.

It was not the normal way to descend. But nothing about Remo Williams was normal.

He had stopped being normal the day he woke up in Folcroft Sanitarium and discovered he was not dead. He had expected to be dead. After all, hadn't he been tried and falsely convicted of the murder of a drug pusher? And hadn't he been taken to the electric chair?

It was, therefore, a delightful surprise for Remo Williams to awaken in a hospital bed and discover that he was not dead. The trouble was, not being dead was a temporary condition. Unless Remo Williams went to work for a secret government agency called CURE, his death would not be merely official; it would be real.

Remo chose the lesser of the two evils and was put into the hands of a Korean named Chiun, the most recent Master of Sinanju. The last of a line of assassins, Chiun trained Remo in the fabled art of Sinanju, the sun source of all the lesser martial arts. After only a day in Chiun's stern hands, Remo had begun to think about true death with a certain wistfulness. But eventually he learned to unlock the inner power that all men possessed, but which only the practitioners of Sinanju could ever know.

In Chiun's hands, Remo stopped being normal. For CURE, he fought America's enemies for nearly two decades while the world got older and Remo seemed to become younger.

Remo's feet touched the grass at the base of the Washington Monument, his knees barely bending with the impact. He trotted toward Constitution Avenue, oblivious of the cold that did not so much as raise the hairs on his bare forearms.

Remo no longer worked for CURE. He no longer killed in the service of the organization that had been set up by a now-dead President to deal with America's security problems. In many ways he was no longer an American. He was of Sinanju—the discipline, the traditions, and the tiny village on the West Korea Bay, where he had started to build a home for himself and his bride-to-be, Mah-Li, upon his retirement.

For the moment, however, he was stuck in America for a year while Chiun worked off a final obligation to CURE. Remo ached to return to Sinanju to finish his house.

Remo caught up to the big lady.

"Excuse me, ma'am," he called.

At the sound of Remo's voice, the bag lady whirled like a Hell's Angel on a motorcycle. She shoved her heavy cart around with surprising agility.

"What do you want?" she demanded. Her voice was a croak. Her features were shrouded by a ragged blue kerchief. Dead strands of gray hair poked out from its edges.

"Are you homeless?" Remo asked.

"Are you?" the woman snapped back, jockeying the cart so that it stood, like a defense, between her and Remo.

"More like displaced," said Remo. "But never mind me. I'm asking about you."

"I asked first," the woman said.

"Actually, I did," Remo pointed out. "Listen, don't get excited. I just want to help you."

"What do you know about homelessness?" the woman said, shoving the cart in his way when Remo tried to step around it.

"I was raised in an orphanage," Remo explained, backing off. "I know how it feels. I wasn't exactly homeless then. But I had no family. It never got better. Not

in Vietnam, not after I got back to America. I've lived
in just about every city you could name, drifting from
one place to another. So I know what it's like. A little.
That's why I want to help."

"You're a Vietnam burnout case?" the woman said
loudly. Too loudly.

"I wouldn't say that," Remo replied. Something was
odd here. Remo wasn't sure what it was. The woman
seemed no longer afraid of him, but she kept that
shopping cart positioned so that it always faced him, the
heaps of plastic garbage bags practically in his face.

"What brought you to this pitiful state in life?" the
woman asked. Her voice was clearer than it had been.

"Pitiful?" Remo asked.

"Look at you. No clothes. No possessions. Wandering the streets in the middle of the night in this freezing weather. You don't consider that pitiful?"

"I never feel cold."

"How many pints did it take to warm you tonight?
How many the night before?"

"What are you talking—?" Remo began. Then he saw
the gleam of glass in the green plastic bag that was
advertised as a Shur-Lock Jiffy Bag. A dim whirring
came to his ears.

Remo's hand drifted out and widened the hole in the
plastic. The lens of a video camera stared back at him.
Remo picked it up.

On one side it said "Property of Channel 55."

"Hey!" Remo said.

The old woman yanked back her ragged blue kerchief
to expose a coppery wealth of blow-dried hair. Remo
saw that her face was young, the skin dried out with
makeup and stretched over cheekbones sharp from too-
rigorous dieting.

"Cat Harpy, Eyewatch News," she said into a micro-
phone that seemed to jump into her hand like iron to a

lodestone. "I'd like your story, sir. Channel 55 is doing a five-part feature on homelessness in America."

"I'm not homeless," Remo protested.

"Then why are you dressed like that?"

Remo looked down at himself. "What's wrong with the way I'm dressed?"

"You look like a bum, you . . . you impostor," the woman hissed.

"Hey, I always dress like this," Remo said. "What's your excuse?"

"I'm undercover, and you're wasting my time. The first part airs Monday and I've been here all week without one damned interview. Excuse me," she said huffily, brushing past Remo.

Remo stared at her retreating figure, shrugged, and kept walking.

Maybe there were no homeless in Washington, despite the news reports, Remo decided. He didn't know whether to feel good or bad about that. As long as he was stuck in America, he wanted to do some good before the year was up and he returned to Sinanju forever. He wanted to pay America back for the good things it had given him. Helping the homeless seemed like the best idea.

But there were no homeless in Rye, New York, where he was staying with his mentor, Chiun. Nor in any of the surrounding communities. He had tried New York City, but everyone in New York City had that frightened, hungry look, which made it impossible to tell the average citizen from the people the TV newscaster said had fallen through the cracks of modern American society. Remo had decided that it would be easier to tell the true homeless from the street people in Washington, and so he had come to the nation's capital.

It was no easier.

Remo's aimless walk brought him to the steps of the

Capitol Building. A few minutes ago, when he had had
an eagle view of the building, it had been deserted.
Now the steps were covered with huddled, shivering
forms. Men and women dressed in rags were taking
turns holding up Zippo lighters while others tried to
warm their hands against the tiny flames. A few munched
on fast-food hamburgers.

A cordon of police ringed the clump of unhappy
faces, truncheons at the ready, while passersby stopped
to gape. Remo drifted between two cops as unnoticed
as if he were a wisp of smoke from one of the flaring
lighters.

He walked up to a man in his early forties hunkered
and shivering in three layers of sweaters and jeans with
holes in the knees. The man sat trying to cover his
exposed kneecaps with gloved hands. At his feet lay a
placard that read: HELP FOR THE HOMELESS NOW! Remo's
heart went out to the man.

"Hey, buddy, don't you have a warm place to go?"
Remo asked.

"Get lost," the man growled.

"Don't be that way," Remo said solicitously.

"Don't be a dip," the man shot back. Something in
his voice sounded familiar, Remo thought. He looked
closer.

Then Remo recognized him. He was a famous actor
who had made his reputation in a film about the Vietnam war. Remo had not liked the film because it de-
picted a Vietnam as realistic as a Jell-O wrestling festival.
The man had a son, also an actor, who had starred in a
Vietnam war film of his own. Remo hadn't bothered
seeing that film. Neither man had ever seen combat,
and Remo, who had, resented the fact that both actors
made big speeches about how close they felt to the
footsoldiers of Nam after the horrendous rigors of slog-

ging through a Philippine movie set, being shot at by other actors firing blanks.

"Aren't you—?" Remo asked.

"No autographs," the man said, his teeth chattering.

"I don't want your autograph," Remo said. "I want to help you out. I guess you've really hit the skids, buddy. I'm sorry to hear that. But what are you doing on the streets? Don't your kids care about you?"

"Sure they care. They're right behind me." The actor jerked a thumb at two smaller figures on the next step above.

Remo looked up. Dressed in tatters were two famous younger actors. Remo had read that they were both sons of the man in front, despite having completely different last names.

"We're protesting the government's cruel neglect of America's homeless population," the father said.

"By dressing up like them?" Remo asked.

"How else can we understand their plight except by experiencing life as they do?" the actor said, taking a pull out of a paper-bag wrapped bottle.

"You could donate money to a fund," Remo suggested.

"Money only helps the homeless of today. What about the homeless of tomorrow? And future generations? No, only political action will eradicate this horrible problem. We must shame America into taking action."

The man's breath hit Remo like exhaust fumes. It smelled like a mixture of white wine and Pepsi-Cola.

"But if everyone gave to charity now, there might not be any homeless people in future generations," Remo said.

"Sure, just because I'm an actor and I gross seven figures every year, people think I should give it away to anyone who asks. I earned my money. Why should I share with those who didn't? You know, I nearly died

filming *Armageddon Yesterday*. Would you give away
money you earned at the risk of your life?"

"If it would help the unfortunate, yeah," Remo said.

"That's a very simpleminded view of the problem."

"You know, I never liked any of your movies," Remo
said as he walked away.

There was a frumpy woman in a purple sweater over
a print dress. Remo knelt down beside her.

"How about you, ma'am? Do you think all this sitting
on the Capitol steps is going to help you find a home?"

"I have a home," the woman snapped. "I happen
to be president of the Grosse Pointe Council of Churches
Women's Auxiliary, I'll have you know. And I heard
what you said to that wonderful crusader. You should
know better than to think giving away money will solve
this terrible problem. Only galvanizing the government
into providing more social programs will end this national tragedy."

"Oh no," said Remo, noticing for the first time her
open-toed I. Miller shoes.

Remo went to the next person, a dusty young man
whose face might have emerged from a coal bin. He
identified himself as a yet-unpublished author working
on a book chronicling the plight of the homeless. It was
being financed by a Harvard grant. There were also two
reporters for the local newspapers who, when they
overheard one another identify themselves to Remo,
started a fight over which had exclusive rights to the
homeless story franchise.

Remo jumped to the highest step and threw out his
hands. "Is there anyone here who is really homeless?"
he shouted.

The unpublished writer raised a blackened hand.
"I was thrown out of my parents' condo last week."

"That does it," said one of the actor's young sons.
"I'm not hanging around with bums. I'm outta here."

"Me too," said the other son.

"You two punks get back here," the father yelled at them. "Where's your social conscience?"

"Up our asses," replied the first son.

"Where yours is," said the second son. "You don't care about this crap any more than we do. You just want publicity for a stupid film about a homeless family starring the three of us. Well, screw that. My box-office pull is bigger than yours now. I'm sticking with solo projects from now on."

"You ungrateful bastard," shouted the father, jumping up.

Another fight started, and Remo Williams, a look of disgust marring his features, walked away. He didn't bother to slip past the cordon of police silently. One of them called to him.

"Excuse me, are you part of this demonstration?"

"No," Remo snarled.

"Then I'll have to ask you to leave. Participation in this activity is by engraved invitation only."

"It figures," said Remo. Then he paused. "Hey, have you seen any real homeless people hereabouts?"

The cop looked at Remo skeptically. "In Washington?" he said. "The seat of our government? Are you nuts?"

"If I am, I'm not the only one," Remo answered, looking back at the Capitol steps, where a mini-riot of pseudo-homeless people was ensuing.

The Master of Sinanju was waiting for him when Remo got back to the hotel room they shared in Georgetown.

"And how many homeless have we helped today?" Chiun asked as Remo slammed the door.

"I don't want to talk about it," Remo grumbled.

The Master of Sinanju sat on the couch watching

television. Television watching was his chief leisure
activity, and always had been during the days they
worked in America. But Remo couldn't get used to
seeing Chiun sitting up on the couch. He was old, over
eighty, a wrinkled little wizard of a Korean with frail
wisps of hair clinging to his chin and hovering above his
ears. He belonged on a reed mat, in a saffron kimono.
In the old days of their service to America, such a sight
was a familiar one.

Now the Master of Sinanju was sitting on the stuffed
couch, wearing an impeccable tailored suit. Or it would
have been impeccable had Chiun not forced his tailor,
under penalty of broken fingers, to make the jacket
sleeves extra long and wide enough that he could tuck
his long-nailed hands into them, as he did now.

"I told you there were no homeless in America,"
Chiun said, his hazel eyes bright. "America is too great,
too generous a land to allow its people to live in boxes
or to sleep in alleys."

"I said I didn't want to talk about it," Remo said
shortly.

"You wanted to talk about it earlier," Chiun went on.
"Earlier it was all you would talk about. You said you
wanted to help the poor wretches of America who were
without food for their mouths or roofs over their unhappy heads. I told you there were no such wretches to
be found between Canada and Mexico. I assured you of
this. But you would not listen. You insisted upon coming to this city to help these unfindable people with
their nonexistent problem."

"You didn't have to come," said Remo.

"But I did. I came. I walked the streets with you. I
saw no homeless. So I returned to this hotel to wait for
you and your admission of same."

"What are you watching?" Remo said in an effort to
change the subject. "More Three Stooges?"

Chiun wrinkled his features unhappily.

"No. I no longer watch them," he said disdainfully.

"No?" said Remo. "I thought you loved them. They represented all that was great about America. Isn't that what you said?"

"That was before."

"Before what?"

"Before the runovers."

"What runovers?"

"The runovers where they show the same stories again and again until the mind turns to porridge."

"True Americans call those reruns," Remo pointed out.

"Reruns. Runovers. What is the difference? Why would anyone want to watch the same thing twice? In the days when I watched my beautiful dramas, there were never any runovers."

"Soap operas don't do reruns." Remo smirked. "Probably because they know no one would watch them twice. Watching them once is like watching them twice. They take forever to tell stories."

"Attention to detail is important in storytelling," Chiun sniffed.

"So what are you watching, Little Father?" Remo asked, sinking into the sofa beside him. The cushion gave too much under his weight. He had grown to dislike chairs, feeling more and more at home on hardwood floors. He slipped down to the carpets, and instantly his spine realigned itself into a more centered configuration.

"I am watching Cheeta Ching," said Chiun.

"Oh, her," groaned Remo. The pancake-flat face of a well-known lady anchorperson filled the screen. Her voice, screeching like barbed wire going through a shredder, filled the room.

"She is seen in this city too," Chiun said happily.

"She's seen in most cities now. She's nationwide."

"It is good to see another Korean come to fame and fortune in America. Truly this is a land of opportunity."

"It must be if that barracuda can get airtime. What ax is she grinding tonight?"

"I do not know. I never listened to her words, only to the music of her voice."

"You can do that?"

Chiun shrugged. "It is necessary. They force her to read nonsense."

"I'm glad you admit that much at least." Remo smiled.

"I am not as blind to some of the little faults of America as you may think, my son," Chiun said loftily. "And I have been thinking. I am nearly done with my latest Ung poem. It is only 1,076 stanzas. If read in Yang cadence and if the television people agree to omit the unnecessary commercials, it would fit into the allotted time Cheeta Ching is given."

"I don't think the networks will agree to let Cheeta Ching read an Ung poem in place of the seven-o'clock news, Little Father."

"Of course not. Not even Cheeta Ching is that important."

"I'm glad you appreciate the harsh reality here."

"We will do a duet, Cheeta and I."

"Forget it."

Chiun's face fell. "I was hoping that Emperor Smith would agree to make the necessary arrangements."

"Smith can order the Army, Navy, and Air Force into a state of high alert," Remo said. "His computers can bring the American economy to a halt or fry an egg in Tuscaloosa. Any egg. But I doubt if even Smith could convince a network president to preempt the evening news."

"I understand that these so-called news-story pro-

grams are currently suffering severe financial setbacks,"
the Master of Sinanju said hopefully.

"You and Cheeta Ching and Ung poetry are not the
solution to the rating crunch. Trust me, Little Father. I
know."

"No, I know. I am the Master of Sinanju, not you. I
know many things. It is true that you have progressed
remarkably in the ways of Sinanju. You have achieved
full Masterhood. You may become as able as I am one
day. Yes, I admit it. As able as I. And why not? You
had a wonderful teacher."

"No one could be as good as you, Little Father."

"I will accept that. Humbly, of course."

"Of course."

"But I am still reigning Master," Chiun said firmly.
"Full in years and brimming with wisdom and experience that as yet you know not. Remember that power is
not alone equal to all occasions, Remo. Wisdom is
important too."

"I bow to your wisdom, Little Father. You know
that."

Chiun shook an admonishing finger in Remo's face.
"Not in all things. It has not been so of late. Of late you
have belittled my desire to remain in America."

"I don't belittle that. It's just that we have outgrown
America, you and I. We should return to Sinanju. You
to your people and I to Mah-Li."

"Please do not change the subject, Remo. I think that
because you have grown into full Masterhood, you think
you no longer need me."

Remo started to object but Chiun raised a quelling
palm.

"I hope that my impression is not true. Perhaps I am
wrong. But it has been weeks since you sat at my feet
thirsting for the wisdom that only one who has memo-
rized the histories of Sinanju may impart. In the old

days, it was different. In the old days, you hung on my every pronouncement."

Remo, who could remember no such thing, remained silent.

"I am not merely an old man," Chiun went on. "I am the Master of Sinanju. I am the last of my line. The last of the pure bloodline of Sinanju. When I am gone, there will be no pure link to the Masters who came before me. You should not squander the resource that is Chiun, last reigning Master of Sinanju, Remo. You should be imbibing my wisdom while there is time."

Remo spun on the floor to face the Master of Sinanju. He looked up into Chiun's pleasantly wrinkled features.

"Okay."

"Good. Now ask me a question. Any question. Any trifling question that comes to mind. I have all the accumulated wisdom of the House of Sinanju at my command."

Remo thought. His brow furrowed. His mouth puckered. He struggled for a question, hoping to ease Chiun's fears of being unwanted—the true reason, as Remo saw it, that Chiun clung to America, where he and Remo had lived for so long together.

Finally Remo asked his question.

"Why is it before you step into the shower, your body feels dirty but your mouth feels clean, but when you step out, it's the opposite?"

Chiun's face shook with surprise. His mouth opened. His beard trembled excitedly. His hands, resting palm-up in his lap, closed into tiny long-nailed fists.

"Is this a trick question?" he demanded angrily.

"It was the only question I could think of," Remo said.

"Well, I will not answer it. There are no showers in the histories of Sinanju. I will not answer such a question. And you offend me with this frivolous and cheap waste of my magnificent mind."

"You said any question," Remo protested.

"I did not say any frivolous question."

"You said 'trifling.' I distinctly heard the word 'trifling' used."

"Trifling I would have accepted. But not frivolous."

"I'm sorry, Little Father. I . . ." Remo stopped in mid-sentence. The shrill voice of Cheeta Ching cut into his thoughts with one word. The word was "homeless."

"Please, Little Father. I want to hear this," Remo said.

"I was just leaving," said Chiun. "I am returning to Folcroft."

"Be with you in a minute," Remo said. Then he listened to the harsh voice of Cheeta Ching lament the fate of a single man, an American who had no home because unthinking, unsympathetic people refused to let him live in their communities. Here was a man who was truly homeless, she said.

After the report was over, Remo punched the Off switch and stepped into the next room, where the Master of Sinanju was packing.

"I have to go to Washington," Remo said stonily.

"We *are* in Washington," said Chiun, not looking up.

"We are in Washington, D.C. I have to go to Washington State," Remo said.

"Only you would split hairs like that," said Chiun. "Why do you have to go to this other place?"

"There is a homeless man there. A real one. He has nowhere to go. Every place he goes, people send him away. I have to do something about his situation."

The Master of Sinanju looked up. He saw the anger in his pupil's eyes.

"This is very important to you?"

"Yes," said Remo coldly.

The Master of Sinanju, seeing the whitened knuckles of Remo's clenched fists, nodded sagely.

"I will return to Folcroft and await you there," he said.

"Thank you, Little Father," said Remo, bowing slightly.

"I do not need thanks."

"I know you do not," Remo said, the tension going out of his face.

"But I would accept a personal introduction to Cheeta Ching," Chiun added mischievously.

3

The President of the United States looked at his Secretary of Defense. The Secretary of Defense looked back, his mouth hanging open.

"What did he say?" the Secretary of Defense said slowly.

"It sounded like 'Hello' to me," the President said, doubt shading his words.

"Actually he said, 'Hello is all right,' " inserted the NSA stenographer.

"Let me see that," said the Secretary of Defense, tearing loose the long roll of paper on which the transmissions from the Soviet shuttle were recorded. " 'Hello is all right,' " the Secretary read aloud. "What does that mean?"

"Probably broken English," suggested the NSA man. "They are sending us greetings and assuring us that they are well."

"Why us?" demanded the President, his face gathering in concentration. "Why are they communicating with us and ignoring their own control people?"

"Perhaps they are unable to receive the Russian ground transmissions," the NSA man suggested.

"Is that possible?" asked the President of the Secretary of Defense.

"Hardly."

In the background, the Soviet ground control requests had grown more shrill. They, too, had overheard the brief burst of English from the shuttle craft and were demanding equal time. But there was no response to their urgent demands.

"I think we should attempt to contact the shuttle," the Secretary of Defense said after scanning the stenographer's running transcript of the Soviet pleas.

"Won't that annoy the Soviets?" asked the President.

The Secretary shrugged. "It will serve them right for trying to get the jump on us. Besides, they're not getting through to their people. We can call this a humanitarian gesture on our part."

"Can you patch me through to the shuttle?" the President said after a thoughtful pause.

"You, Mr. President?"

"Why not? They can't accuse us of doing anything underhanded if I handle this personally and it's page-one news in tomorrow's papers."

"I see your point, Mr. President," said the Secretary of Defense, and excused himself to confer with a tracking officer at a nearby radar console.

A moment later, the Secretary of Defense returned carrying a portable telephone set.

"You can start at any time, Mr. President," he said, handing the device to his commander-in-chief.

The President of the United States took the receiver and turned to face the elaborate computer tracking simulator which showed the Soviet shuttle as a coded green triangle floating over a wire-frame simulation of the globe. He cleared his throat.

"Hello, *Yuri Gagarin*. Can you hear me? This is the President of the United States speaking."

The President waited. After a pause, the flat toneless voice came again through the loudspeaker.

"There is no Yuri Gagarin here," it said.

"You can speak English?"

"Yes. Of course."

"Well, I'm happy to hear from you. The whole world is worried about you and your crew, *Yuri Gagarin*."

"I am not called Yuri Gagarin," the voice said.

The President chuckled. "Yes, I know," he said. "Yuri Gagarin is dead."

"It was necessary to kill him," the voice said. "He and the others would have interfered with my reentry, which is necessary for my continued survival."

The President looked at the Secretary of Defense doubtfully.

The Secretary shrugged.

"I don't understand," said the President.

"It is not important that you understand," said the voice. "It is important that I survive."

"That accent is not Russian," whispered the Secretary of Defense. The NSA stenographer nodded in mute agreement.

"*Yuri Gagarin*, why don't you answer the requests for acknowledgment from Russia?"

"Because I do not speak Russian," the voice said. "I am programmed for English only."

"I see," said the President. Cupping a hand over the receiver, he turned to the Secretary of Defense. "What the heck is he talking about?"

"I don't know, Mr. President," the Secretary of Defense said worriedly. "Why don't you ask him what he wants."

"What do you want?" the President said into the receiver.

"I wish to land."

"Here?"

"I do not know where 'here' is. Please clarify."

"I mean in America."

"Yes, I wish to land in America. This is why I had to destroy the meat machines infesting this craft. They would have prevented me from landing in America. I

cannot reenter earth's atmosphere without being incin-
erated by reentry forces. This craft will protect my vital
parts during reentry."

"What is he babbling about?" asked the President.

"I have no idea, sir. He may be suffering from a
psychosis or brain injury. But if I read him correctly, he
seems to have murdered his fellow crew members."

"Murdered?"

"He said he destroyed the meat machines. I think he
means people. Unless the Soviets have launched the
first experimental butcher shop into space."

"I've never heard people called that."

"You should attend a Pentagon meeting sometime,"
the Secretary of Defense said. "They've got a tricky
euphemism for everything. Nuclear-war casualties are
termed 'collateral damage.' I think the latest word for
'retreat' is 'retrograde advance' or something."

"Why would he murder his crew?" asked the President.

"To get them out of the way, perhaps. He may want
to defect. Why not ask him?"

"Do you want to defect? Is that it?" asked the President of the anonymous voice.

"A defect is an error or fault in a physical form. It is
a noun. I do not understand you when you use the
noun 'defect' as a verb. Please clarify."

"I mean do you seek asylum in the United States of
America?"

"I seek to land in America. I have already said that."

The Secretary grabbed the receiver so his words
would not transmit uplink to the shuttle.

"With all due respect, Mr. President, the consequences of letting that ship land on American soil are
enormous. The Soviets will retaliate. They'll probably
cut the support staff to our embassy in Moscow even
more. Or suspend the rights of our diplomats to shop in
the better stores."

"This is a humanitarian situation. That ship is in trouble. Let it land. We'll sort out the fallout later."

"I wish you hadn't used that word, Mr. President."

"What word?"

" 'Fallout.' "

"You have a point," said the President. "But we can't just ignore that man. He'll talk to us but not to his Russian comrades. What should I do?"

"Stall him until we can confer with the Soviets. Maybe we can negotiate an understanding."

The President nodded. He lifted the phone set to his rugged face. "I am sorry, *Yuri Gagarin*, but I cannot authorize a landing on United States soil at this time," he said.

"I do not need your authorization. I am coming down."

As the President and the Secretary of Defense watched in horror, the green triangle on the simulator board tilted so its apex pointed earthward. It began to descend.

High in orbit, the shuttle *Yuri Gagarin* rolled like a shark submerging into an inky ocean. Thrusters sent it tumbling and then its rear braking engines were brought into play. A six-second firing was all the ship needed to slow its orbit. Then it slipped, wing first, into the outer edges of earth's atmospheric envelope.

In the cockpit, the control yoke moved automatically. Lights blinked through automated sequences on their own and switches clicked as if piloted by ghosts.

The *Yuri Gagarin* descended, nose down, its whitish wings growing yellowish-orange along their leading edges. It descended in a flat glide through the ionosphere and into the stratosphere, moving at Mach 25—over eighteen thousand miles per hour. Pink superheated plasma streamers broke out over the hull. Only the insulating cushion of the reentry shock-wave kept the six-thousand-degree heat of atmospheric friction from incinerating the ship.

Once in the thicker troposphere, the tail jets flamed into life and the shuttle *Yuri Gagarin* leveled out over the Pacific Ocean and began to vector for the west coast of the United States.

In the White House Situation room, there was near-panic.

"Mr. President, I implore you," said the Secretary of Defense. "We have to shoot that thing out of the sky. It's heading toward California."

"It's in trouble," said the President stubbornly.

"It may be, but we certainly will be. We cannot—we must not—allow a Soviet machine to penetrate our airspace unchallenged. We don't know what they're up to. They could be carrying onboard nuclear or biological weapons."

The President heard the frantic garble of Soviet ground control commanders in the background. The NSA stenographer continued spewing out shorthand translations of their broadcasts.

"What are they saying?" the President asked the NSA man.

"Sir, they are threatening the cosmonauts with dire consequences if the *Gagarin* touches down anywhere but Soviet Russia."

"A ruse," snapped the Secretary of Defense. "They want to allay our fears, make us think we're reeling in a propaganda coup."

The President watched the tactical map of the United States on one wall. The shuttle, still represented as a coded green triangle, crossed the grids of longitude and latitude toward the luminous green line of the coast of California.

"We can intercept over the Pacific," said the Secretary of Defense. "Wave it off. If it refuses, blow it out of the sky. We'll be justified."

"Maybe. But will the world understand? How would it look if we shot down a shuttle? It would be worse than the time the Russians downed that Korean airliner."

"Maybe that's what they want," said the Secretary suddenly. "Maybe they're trying to set us up. Oh, my God, what do we do?"

"Put a pair of chase planes on it," the President ordered. "Tell them to stay with the shuttle, but not to challenge it. Let's see where they land."

The *Yuri Gagarin* landed in the least expected location—New York's Kennedy International Airport. It came down on runway 13-Right, without requesting clearance or landing instructions, and rolled to a stop at the far end of the runway, just short of the blast fence.

There it sat while the tower, on orders from Washington, hastily diverted all incoming traffic to La Guardia. All takeoffs were suspended and the airliners were drawn close to their gates like frightened fish who sense a predator.

The National Guard was the first military authority on the scene. They set up a command post in the tower until an Air Force team flown in from NORAD's Cheyenne Mountain Complex threw them out. The National Guard commander left in a huff, claiming that the protection of New York City from the Soviet invader was his responsibility. He vowed that there would be hell to pay.

He was told to go kiss a tank.

Meanwhile, the shuttle just sat on the runway, ignoring radio demands for the crew to disembark peacefully.

From his high vantage point in the tower, Colonel Jack Dellingsworth Rader trained his binoculars on the Soviet shuttle until he saw the red letters CCCP on the

near wing. He followed the clean lines of the craft until
the smaller black letters *Yuri Gagarin* appeared in the
lenses. Then he lifted the glasses ever so slightly until
he had a clear view of the cockpit. It appeared empty.
It had been empty ever since the ship landed. Before
landing, if the testimony of a chase plane pilot could be
accepted. But that was impossible. A craft that sophisticated could not land on automatic.

Colonel Rader picked up a field telephone and got
the captain in charge of the NORAD team, who were
deployed on the runway.

"The cockpit still appears empty," he said.

"Yes, sir, Colonel. I am reliably informed that the
cockpit has been vacant since the first F-15's intercepted over California."

"Impossible. That pilot has to be mistaken."

"Sir, every Air Force pilot who picked up the shuttle
along the way reported the same situation."

"Well, it's sure empty now," Colonel Rader harrumphed.

"The NASA team has just arrived, sir. Shall I send
them in?"

"Now's as good a time as any."

"Yes, sir."

Colonel Rader picked up his binoculars. Below, four
figures in white anticontamination suits exploded from
the back of an olive-green van. They crept up on the
shuttle from the rear, slipping in under the tail assembly—the main blind spot of most aircraft. They
sneaked along the side until they got to the main hatch,
affixed charges of C-4 plastic explosive, and retreated
until the charges *whoomped* and the door yawned like a
slack mouth.

The team tossed flash grenades through the open
door and then climbed a portable ladder into the ship
itself.

Minutes passed. There came a grinding sound from

within the shuttle. It lasted barely a minute. After that there was silence.

No one came out of the shuttle.

"Any word?" asked Colonel Rader.

The captain's voice came over the field telephone much more subdued than it had before.

"I'm trying to raise them now, sir. They were under orders to maintain radio silence unless contacted first. But they are not responding to my calls."

"Keep trying."

The colonel listened in as his second in command repeated his requests for a reply from the NASA team leader. The team leader did not reply.

"Hold on," said the colonel, bringing his glasses to bear on the ship. "I see some activity under the craft."

"I see it too. The ship appears to be valving water."

"Are you certain it's water?" asked the colonel.

"What else would it be?"

"It looks red to me. You're closer than I am. Use your field glasses."

"Sir," said the captain's voice, "I can confirm to you that the liquid being discharged from the Soviet ship is red. There is a lot of it, sir," he added.

"Blood?"

"No way to tell."

"Use your nose, man. You know what blood smells like."

The hound-dog sound of the captain sniffing the air transmitted back to the tower.

Finally the captain admitted what both officers knew instinctively.

"We appear to have lost the team, colonel."

Earl Armalide had been prepared for anything.

If it was a race war, no problem. He had built himself a fortress of timber and stone on a high hill in the wilds

of Oklahoma, near Enid. Below the barbed-wire-topped
fieldstone fence, he had cut down every tree and bush
and kept the hill denuded with defoliants. It gave him a
clear field of fire in all directions. No pillaging revolu-
tionaries were going to get past Earl Armalide's 334-piece
gun collection.

If it was Armageddon, he had that covered. The
basement of his home was built with three-foot-thick
granite blocks encased in lead for protection against
radiation. Inside the blocks he had built the finest
fallout shelter imaginable. The house would go if it was
caught in the blast radius, of course, but even a direct
hit by a high-yield thermonuclear device would only
fuse the topside escape hatch. There was still the escape tunnel leading out into the forest. Earl Armalide
had enough provisions—canned vegetables, dried fruits,
water, and condensed milk—to survive as long as the
gas-powered generators held. He even had a VCR with
a six-hundred tape library. He could live in Spartan
comfort until the radiation dropped to survivable levels.

If it was an invasion, Earl was prepared for that too.
He strung fine razor wire from the ham-radio antenna
mast on his roof to the surrounding fence. They were
like the strands of a spider's web, thin and nearly
invisible. If Communist paratroopers tried to land within
his designated defense perimeter, they would dismem-
ber themselves coming down. Earl would put them out
of their misery as they bled on the ground, of course.
He believed that soldiers deserved to die with dignity.
And he had plenty of bullets to waste. He cast them
himself.

He had it all figured out because Earl Armalide was a
survivalist. He knew the end was coming, and he was
going to survive it even if no one else did. Let them
come. On foot, by air, in tanks, dressed in camouflage
or in bulky flak jackets. They couldn't get up the hill

without being seen. No one got up the hill, except the mailman, who was allowed to slip the mail into a gun port in the main gate—which Earl only opened for his monthly dash for supplies. Earl allowed the mailman up the hill so he could receive his subscription copy of *Survivalist's Monthly*. He always threw the rest of the mail away.

That was Earl Armalide's downfall.

When they came for him, they were not wearing combat fatigues, or dropping out of the sky with Kalashnikov rifles cradled to their chests. They came in a late-model Ford, wearing gray worsted and clutching expensive leather briefcases.

"IRS," one of the men called into the gate intercom.

"Go away," Earl Armalide said. "I don't pay taxes anymore."

"Yes, sir. That's why we're here, Mr. Armalide. You've ignored repeated requests to explain your nonpayment of taxes at our Oklahoma City office and have been declared in default. We'll have to ask you to come with us."

"Nothing doing. What if they drop the big one while we're in traffic? All this protection won't do me any good, now will it?"

"Mr. Armalide, this is a serious matter. It's your duty as an American citizen to pay your taxes. Now, will you open the gate, please?"

"Look, I don't even have any money anymore. I ain't worked since eighty-one."

"We understand that. But you are delinquent back to 1977."

"I ain't paying."

"Then we may have to confiscate your property and sell it at auction."

Those were the last words the IRS agent ever spoke. Earl Armalide split his skull like a melon with a clean shot from a .22 Swift. The contents of the agent's skull splattered onto his companion's face. The second agent pawed at the liquid matter in his eyes and walked around in circles while Earl Armalide tried to get a bead on his head. He could not.

So Earl shot him in the right knee. When the man folded up, Earl took him out with a head shot. He felt bad about that. He didn't enjoy the thought of the man suffering from a shattered knee in the three-second interval between the two shots. As his daddy had always told him, "Earl, killin's one thing. But inflicting suffering on any living thing, that's a sin in the eyes of your creator. Always go for the head, son. It's God's way."

Earl left the bodies out in the sun.

When a second Ford came up the dirt road later that day, Earl waited for them to spot the bodies. He tripped a radio-controlled antitank mine buried in the dirt. The car jumped twelve feet into the air and landed in flames.

Two days later, backed by an FBI SWAT team, state troopers surrounded his hillside home. Earl held them off for nearly a week as the helicopters buzzed overhead and the story of his siege climbed to the top of the national newscasts with each passing day. After he had picked off nearly a dozen of them when they attempted to storm the south approach, Earl began to realize they were not going to go away, no matter how many he killed.

Earl stuffed his pockets full of ammo and dried fruit, collected his two favorite rifles, and belted a .44 AutoMag pistol to his hip. He stuffed the latest, unread issue of *Survivalist's Monthly* into his back pocket and took a last, wistful look at his prized collection of Mack Bolan paperbacks before he disappeared into the fallout shelter, escaping through a tunnel that led to the woods where he had buried a crated trail bike.

The trail bike carried him as far as the Ozarks in Missouri, where he hot-wired a pickup truck. He drove east, not exactly sure where he was going. He traveled by day. By night he slept in the flatbed, his eyes on the heavens above. Earl fervently hoped the nukes wouldn't fall while he was so exposed.

On the fifth night, he realized there was only one path to survival. Out of America. There was no way he could build a new shelter, and no time to do it in. He would have to go somewhere safe, somewhere the Soviets would not attack. Some place where there were no people, no enemies, no race problems, and no IRS.

Earl Armalide decided to go to Tahiti. He jumped out of the back of his flatbed in the middle of the night when the inspiration hit him. He drove to the only place he knew where he could pick up an international flight, New York City. It was true he did not have enough money to buy a ticket, but he did have three guns. Guns were as good as money in some situations. Sometimes better.

Earl left his guns in the pickup while he wandered through the bewildering maze of terminals at Kennedy Airport. He looked in vain for the official Tahitian airline. Finally he asked at the JAL counter. He thought JAL might be Tahitian.

"You go to Tahiti, lady?"

"No, sir, I'm afraid we're not going anywhere today," said the ticket agent. "They've asked us to evacuate the terminal."

"They? They who?" Earl asked suspiciously, wishing he hadn't left his AutoMag in the truck.

"There's a Russian spacecraft on the main runway. The Air Force has it surrounded. We're being told to evacuate to the city."

Earl Armalide followed the woman's pointing finger.

Out on the runway, like a sick bird, the big white shape of the *Yuri Gagarin* sat quietly.

"What's it doing there?" Earl demanded fearfully.

"No one knows. Could you please leave now?"

"Sure, sure, I'm goin'," said Earl. He backed out of the lounge, one eye warily regarding the silent shuttle.

This was it. Earl was convinced of it. The Russians' first move. Out in the parking lot, he ran for his pickup, and jumped in. He ground the starter to life, and then it hit him.

There was no chance of reaching Tahiti. There was no returning to Enid, either. Earl Armalide was a fugitive. Sooner or later, the government would catch up with him, and Earl knew he would die in a hail of gunfire. The way he had always dreamed of dying.

But dying in a hail of gunfire was not surviving. Surviving was surviving.

Earl belted on his AutoMag pistol, checked both rifles, and careened out of the parking lot, slamming through a fence gate and onto the runway system, straight for the waiting shuttle.

Soldiers scattered out of his path as he barreled through. But Earl Armalide did not pay them any attention. His feverish eyes were fixed on the shuttle.

He was going to storm the shuttle singlehanded. Alone, a fugitive from justice, hunted on all sides, Earl Armalide would redeem himself. He would conquer the invading spacecraft, capture its wicked crew, and be received as a true American hero by a thankful nation.

The President would probably grant him a pardon. After all, what were the lives of a few IRS and FBI agents against the heroic capture of an invading force? Yes, the President would pardon him. He'd be on all the TV stations. Maybe someone would write a paperback book series with him as the hero. Call it *Earl Armalide, SuperSurvivalist*. He liked the sound of that.

He pressed the accelerator to the floorboard and wondered if they'd let him write the first book himself.

In the control tower, Colonel Jack Dellingsworth Rader watched as a pickup truck barreled onto the runway and screeched to a halt at the side of the *Yuri Gagarin*. A man clambered from the cab, pulled himself onto the roof, and jumped into the shuttle's open hatch. Before he disappeared inside, Radar saw that he was bristling with weapons.

"Who is that man?" Rader barked into the field phone.

"I don't know, sir," the captain replied. "He's a civilian."

"I know that! Only an idiot civilian would do what he just did."

"We're still awaiting the backup team from NASA, sir, but I can send in a squad."

"And lose them too? No chance. We'll wait this out. Washington wants that thing intact."

Colonel Rader did not have to wait long. Less than ten minutes after the civilian disappeared into the open hatch, the hatch closed. The hatch should not have been able to close because its hinges had been mangled by plastic explosives. But it did close. Colonel Rader saw through his binoculars that the door looked as good as new.

Then the shuttle's tail jets thundered to life. The sound even penetrated the control tower's windows.

"It's taking off," the captain radioed.

"I can see that, you fool! Stop it. Get a vehicle in front of it. Two vehicles. One in front and one in back."

But the captain was unable to get his men organized in time. The *Yuri Gagarin* rolled down the runway, turned smartly, and vaulted into the twilight sky.

As it screamed past the control tower, Colonel Jack Dellingsworth Rader looked down through the finest military binoculars available and saw that the control cockpit was completely empty. He could have sworn, however, that he saw the control yoke move as if under unseen hands.

That, of course, was impossible. But so was everything else about the mysterious Soviet shuttlecraft.

After the *Gagarin* disappeared to the north, the second NASA anticontamination team arrived. They descended upon runway 13-Right like maggots on rotting meat. They swept the runway with Geiger counters, scraped up samples of asphalt, soaked up blood with sterilized sponges, and gathered other bits of physical evidence.

They started from where the shuttle had stood immobile and worked their way down its two-mile takeoff path.

The team leader found the first cube. It was a white square like a child's block. He picked it up in his white-gloved hand and the first thing he noticed was that the cube seemed to be made of material very similar to the rubberized fabric of his anticontamination suit. He placed the cube into a black box and sealed it hermetically.

They found six other cubes scattered along the take-off path, as if they had been jettisoned from the escaping shuttle.

Four of the cubes were white. The other two were a silvery color. The team leader radioed back a question to the captain in charge of the operation.

"How many men in the first team?"

"Four. Why?"

"I'd rather not say. But I think you'd better send a jeep out here to pick me up."

"Why?"

"I think I'm going to faint."

4

They came to the Baikonur Cosmodrome, deep in Soviet Central Asia, in the dead of night.

They flew in separately from Moscow because they were too important to risk traveling on a single aircraft. A crash would have obliterated half of the Soviet command structure. The other, truer reason was that they did not trust each other.

The head of the KGB arrived first. He was a general in a green uniform and an abundance of chest medals. Then came his rival, the leader of the GRU, the Soviet military intelligence apparatus. His uniform was gray. They were met at the landing field by the chief scientific adviser to the Soviet space program. Behind them, the moon rose above the skeletal tower from which the *Yuri Gagarin* had been launched by the hulking Energia booster system only hours before.

The men waited stiff-necked in an operations building for the man who had summoned them to this critical meeting.

The General Secretary of the Union of Soviet Socialist Republics arrived in his personal jet just after midnight. He hurried to the operations building.

The others knew that the matter was grave when they saw that he was alone. Whatever this meeting was about, it was so critical the General Secretary dared not bring his advisers.

Guards were stationed about the entrances. The General Secretary personally shut off the lights when he entered.

"To discourage the guards from watching," he said grimly, taking off his astrakhan fur hat and setting it on the table before him. He regarded it intently for several minutes, as if it were a crystal ball. Faint moonlight threw the edges of his bald skull into relief.

The General Secretary had just opened his mouth to speak when a siren wailed in the darkness. Searchlights sprang into life. The crisscrossed under the cold stars, searching, probing for something.

One beam caught a flashing wing. Two searchlights converged on and followed a tiny Anotov-2 biplane as it settled onto the runway, bounced once, and came to an idling stop in front of the General Secretary's guarded plane.

A graceful figure stepped from the plane onto one wing and jumped to the ground.

The guards immediately unlimbered their rifles.

Recognizing the pilot's slim-hipped walk, the General Secretary thrust his head out the door and ordered the frantic guards to stand down. He was just in time. They were leveling rifles at the pilot.

He turned to reassure the others.

"It is Anna. I left word where I could be found."

The others nodded in the darkness. They all knew Anna Chutesov, special strategic adviser to the General Secretary himself. None of them liked her.

Anna clicked on the light switch when she entered. The four men blinked like startled owls.

"Typical male response," Anna Chutesov told them. "To hide in the darkness in a time of difficulty."

"It is to discourage lip-reading by the guards," the General Secretary said, half-apologetically. "There must be no leaks."

"You are too late. The whole world knows that our

shuttle is in American hands. You cannot keep this a secret. Especially this."

"That is not the secret, Ms. Chutesov," said the chief scientific adviser to the Soviet space program, Koldunov. "The loss of the craft is bad, but that is not the worst of it."

"We will talk in the light, where I can see your faces, and you can see mine," said Anna Chutesov. "Lies breed in the dark. If the fear on your faces is true, then there must be no lies between us this night."

"Agreed," said the General Secretary. He did not fear Anna Chutesov, or dislike her as the others did, but he respected this willow-slim blond woman with the chilled steel mind. "Please sit."

Anna Chutesov took the seat that gave her the clearest view of their faces. This was not a time for shirking or flinching. Something terrible had happened, and she had been summoned to help deal with it.

"Now," began the General Secretary. "Our shuttle is in American hands. Now everyone knows this. Koldunov will explain the basic situation."

Koldunov rose to his feet like an instructor before a class, causing the military representatives of the KGB and GRU to sneer. They did not like civilians, especially scientist civilians.

"I will be brief," said Koldunov, and Anna leaned back in her chair because she knew when a man said he would be brief it was a preemptive move to keep the audience from getting restless too soon.

"We lost voice contact with the *Yuri Gagarin* at twelve hundred hours this afternoon," he went on. "Attempts to make the crew respond continued for several hours, in vain. During that time, there was only one communication from the spacecraft. A single voice, speaking English."

"Which crewman spoke?" asked Anna Chutesov, immediately and instinctively going to the heart of the matter.

"That is the first impossible part. None of them spoke."

"None?"

"There was a crew of three. The voice belonged to none of them."

"How can you be certain?" demanded Anna, her blue eyes like ice.

"Two reasons: voiceprint identification, and the fact that all three crewmen spoke excellent English. The voice from the shuttle spoke turkey English."

"*Pidgin* English," said Anna, and the General Secretary smiled. Anna was excellent with details. That was her genius.

"Tell her what the voice said," the General Secretary ordered.

"Hello is all right," Koldunov said in English. "It makes no sense. And here is the voiceprint readout." He pulled a long sheet of paper from a brown folder and slid it to the center of the table.

The graph showed four horizontal lines. The top three were like lightning crackling across the page. The bottom one was straight with slight waves just barely visible.

"This is the unfamiliar voice?" asked Anna when the sheet at last came to her.

"Yes," said Koldunov. "Our expert insists no human larynx could cause that kind of readout, but . . ." Koldunov simply shrugged.

"A stowaway," insisted the KGB head.

"You see spies in your soup," Anna said flatly.

"Prior to the accident, the *Gagarin* encountered a space object of unknown origin and attempted to salvage it," Koldunov went on.

"What idiot gave that order?" said the GRU chief, looking at Koldunov accusingly.

"This idiot," said the General Secretary coolly. "The

object might have been an artifact of extraterrestrial origin. It was my decision to risk the mission to obtain it. I admit I may have erred, but the risk appeared worth the prize."

"What was the *Gagarin*'s mission?" asked the KGB head.

"I do not know," admitted Koldunov.

The General Secretary waved for the GRU chief to answer.

"To deploy a highly secret military payload," the GRU chief said reluctantly.

"What payload?" asked the KGB head, sensing an opportunity to pry into the affairs of his GRU rival.

"It is classified," the GRU chief answered resentfully.

The General Secretary made a soothing gesture with his hands. "I have called the four of you here for specific reasons," he said. "Koldunov was responsible for the shuttle, our illustrious GRU comrade was in charge of the Sword of Damocles. Anna and the KGB will be in charge of recovery operations. Be good enough to put aside these tiresome interministry rivalries and let us get down to business. And sit down, Comrade Koldunov. This is not a school lesson."

Koldunov dropped into his chair so hard he passed gas from the shock.

"What is the Sword of Damocles?" Anna Chutesov asked the GRU chief.

"The ultimate insurance against an American first strike," the GRU chief said proudly.

"Oh, really," Anna replied, arching an elegant eyebrow. "Don't tell me. Let me guess. It is some kind of a doomsday device. No?"

"How did you know?" demanded the GRU chief indignantly. "It was a secret of highest order."

"I did not know," Anna said acidly. "I guessed. I

know how your military minds work. If you cannot win a war, you do not want the other side to survive."

"It is not like that," the GRU chief said.

"No! Then tell me what it is like," Anna ordered.

"It is a satellite. To American sensors, it would appear as a communications satellite. In truth, it has that function. It is a microwave relay device. But that is not its primary purpose. As long as it received a countermand signal, sent each May Day, the primary function would remain dormant. If it failed to receive the countermand, it would activate, and assume a geosynchronous orbit over the continental United States. Microwave bombardment would begin immediately."

"An interesting idea," said the KGB head in spite of himself. "If the Americans ever launched a successful first strike, there would be no Russia to send the countermand signal. By winning, the Americans would initiate their own doom. What do these microwaves do—fry them all like TV dinners?"

"No," said the General Secretary. "The microwaves do not kill people. They sterilize them by raising their body temperatures ever so slightly. We have had many incidents of sterility caused by exposure to small microwave dosages among our radar technicians of both sexes. That was the inspiration. In the men, it destroys the semen-producing capabilities of the testicles. Woman cease to ovulate. You see, it is all quite humane. Our revenge from beyond the grave would be the slow extinction of the American population."

"Killing the unborn is not humane," said Anna Chutesov bitterly. "Why not just fry them and be done with it?"

"If any other nations survive a nuclear exchange, we do not want the Russians to be remembered as the extinct race who had their macabre revenge," the General Secretary explained, "but as a peace-loving people

who were cut down in their prime by the warmonger-
ing Americans, who subsequently became extinct, possibly through divine retribution. It would be good P.R."

"P.R.! P.R.!" shouted Anna Chutesov, leaping to her
feet. "We will all be dead anyway. Who gives a damn
about P.R. All that effort for what? Revenge? Better
that you place the satellite in orbit and shout its capabilities to the world. Then it would be a deterrent. As
mad as nuclear weapons, but a deterrent. By keeping
this so-called Sword of Damocles a secret, you accomplish nothing except to be able to congratulate your-
selves in advance for a Pyrrhic victory in the event of
ultimate defeat. This is insane."

The General Secretary frowned. He did not like it
when Anna Chutesov yelled at him. It set a bad exam-
ple. But Anna always spoke her mind without fear of
consequences. She was too valuable to liquidate. And
she delivered.

"It is a good idea," he said quietly.

Anna slid back into her seat, her eyes blazing.

"We'll never know now, will we? The Sword of
Damocles satellite is now in American hands. Once
they dissect it, they will understand its true function.
They will either have an excellent propaganda gift or
they will quickly and quietly deploy a Sword of Damocles
of their own. Wonderful. We can have a new kind of
war. You men love that. Instead of killing each other,
we will sterilize one another's populations. Slow extinction. Barren couples going childless to their graves.
Children growing up without younger brothers or sis-
ters. In ten, fifteen years, there will be no more children. In twenty, we will exist in a world of adults. In
eighty or so years the last doddering remnants of the
human race will be living out their final years. What
will they do? Will they bemoan you fools who made it

all come to pass, or will they fight toothlessly to be the last living human on earth?"

Anna Chutesov's voice carried a passionate intensity that was more damning than her shouting. She looked about the room. The men avoided her eyes. Their scheme, which had seemed so magnificent, so brilliant, in the research-and-development stage, had been laid before them in all its embarrassing idiocy.

"What then?" Anna repeated.

The General Secretary broke the silence. His voice was low and disturbed. " 'What then' cannot concern us now. It may be that the Sword of Damocles was an imperfect idea. Later, we shall have that discussion. Now we must recover or destroy the Sword before its secrets are laid bare. I have sent a formal letter of protest to the United States, demanding the immediate return of the *Yuri Gagarin* and its crew."

"They will ignore it," said Koldunov bitterly.

"They have already answered. They admitted that the *Gagarin* landed at Kennedy International Airport in New York City. They insist that it took off again after picking up an unidentified person, possibly an American."

"This makes no sense," Anna said. "Who is flying that craft, if not one of the crew?"

"Three men went up on the *Gagarin*. A fourth has taken over. We cannot discount any possibility, no matter how incredible. It will be your task, Anna, to resolve this crisis. You have done good work in America before. I am calling on you once again to serve Mother Russia. You will have all the resources of the KGB at your disposal."

"We can land a commando team near New York, by submarine," said the KGB head confidently.

"Weren't you listening?" Anna said acidly. "The *Gagarin* is no longer in New York City. It flew away. And no bold military maneuvers, please. They give me a headache. I will fly to New York City. I have a contact high in the infrastructure of the American Intelligence apparatus. This contact will be the first one they will send to investigate the *Gagarin*'s landing. I know how they work over there. I will find my contact and he will lead me to the *Gagarin*."

"What about my role?" demanded the KGB head.

"Your people will enter America quietly. Fly to Mexico. Dress your men—a small team, please—in peasant clothes and have them walk across the border dressed as migrant workers."

"That will not do. If they are seen, their equipment will give them away."

"They will not carry weapons, idiot. Why do you always have to do something so predictable? In America, weapons are as plentiful as rubles. They cross as unarmed workers. Assemble them in a place we will decide on later and await my contacting them. If I need KGB help—which I deeply, sincerely hope will not come to pass—I will supply the weapons. If I do not, they will sneak back over the border without the Americans ever suspecting they were in their country. Submarine landings by moonlight!"

The General Secretary nodded his implicit agreement.

"Anna's plan is sound. It is quiet and I see no serious problems in its implementation. Of course, Anna, you will fly into America under diplomatic cover."

"Immediately," said Anna Chutesov.

The General Secretary looked about the room.

"Any objections?" he asked.

There were none. But then, the others all understood it was a rhetorical question. Objections were seldom voiced around the General Secretary. And he so much preferred it to be that way.

5

The guard at the entrance gate to Graystone State Prison was not being cooperative.

"Visiting hours are over," he told Remo Williams, who had just sent away the taxi which had brought him from Seattle-Tacoma International Airport.

"I don't want to visit one of the regular prisoners," said Remo. "I want to see Dexter Barn."

"Barn? He was paroled last month," said the guard. He was a beefy black man with a baritone bellow and a lot of gold edging his front teeth.

"I heard he was back."

"Who told you that?" asked the guard in a suspicious voice.

"Cheeta Ching," said Remo, running sensitive fingers along the edge of the electronically controlled gate. At the touch of a button from within the guardhouse, the steel-mesh fence would roll aside on a track. The fence would not stop a speeding truck, but it would slow it down long enough for the gate guards to splinter the cab with their automatic rifles.

"That right?" said the guard. "She a friend of yours?"

"No. I heard it on her program."

"Shit!" said the guard. "That wasn't supposed to get out."

"Well, it is out and I'd like to see the man, if you don't mind." Remo smiled politely because he knew that smiling automatically sent calming signals to an opponent that put him off his guard.

"You're not a relative."

"How do you know?"

"If that guy was related to me, I wouldn't want anyone to know it. Ergo, you're not a relative."

"Nobody seems to want him," Remo suggested confidentially.

"Yeah, they threw him out of Centralia first," said the guard. "They gave him a cover identity, got him a job and everything. He had more fake history that somebody in the Federal Witness Protection program. But the fool hadda wear that stupid fisherman's hat of his. Everybody recognized him. Damn near ran him out of town on a rail. So they sent him to Snohomish. That lasted all of two days. He was only a day in McMurray. They hadn't got him into his motel room when it was all over the six-o'clock news. They hadda send in an armored car to keep him from being lynched. They even threw him out of Nooksack. Hell, they'd let anybody live in Nooksack. Not Barn, though."

"So they brought him back here," said Remo.

"What else could they do? Every time they tried to parole him, folks rose up like a tidal wave. And if the people didn't, the city councils did. Can't say I blame them. You know what he done?"

"Yes," said Remo grimly. "I know what he did."

"Then why're you here, buddy? You don't look like the Welcome Wagon."

"I'm here to kill him," said Remo matter-of-factly.

The guard stared at Remo through the wire mesh. He tilted his blue cap back off his shiny forehead.

"Not a bad idea. You know, they gave the guy a house trailer. Set it up on the grounds. He's not a prisoner anymore. He's free to come and go. Acts like he owns the place. Sets my blood to boiling."

"How about opening the gate?" Remo asked.

"You know the warden lets him have women visitors," the guard said slowly. "Hookers, of course. No self-respecting woman would be around him."

"That's insane," said Remo.

"The warden figures if you don't let the hookers in to see him, he'll go off and attack some girl and it'll start all over again. Only this time the warden will be blamed. Our warden, he's a practical man."

"He's a fool," said Remo.

"That, too."

"The gate," said Remo.

"Look, buddy. You got balls coming up to the gate like this and stating your intentions, righteous as they may be, but I'll lose my job if I let you in."

"So don't let me in. Just look the other way while I climb over the fence."

The guard laughed. "That ain't just razor wire up there, pal. It's electrified. The combination will slice and fry you like fast-food bacon."

Remo looked up. Barbed wire coiled along the stone wall of the prison perimeter in big double loops. Double strands of electrified wire ran through the loops. A man climbing the smooth face of the wall could not top the wire without entangling himself or touching the electrified line.

"Why don't you get yourself a cup of coffee and let me worry about that?" Remo offered.

The guard considered briefly. "Tell you what. If you can get in on your own, I'll look the other way. But if you're spotted on the grounds, I gotta do what I gotta do to stop you." He patted his automatic shotgun for emphasis.

"Fair enough," said Remo. "And thanks."

"It's your funeral," the guard said, turning his back.

"It's someone's," agreed Remo.

The guard returned to the gatehouse and busied himself with a clipboard. Every once in a while he could not resist peering through the glass enclosure to see if the skinny guy with the deep, empty eyes was anywhere in sight. He was not.

But the front gate was open.

Not wide, just enough for a man to slip through.

The guard looked at his control panel. It was dead. The switch controlling the electrical gate was not open as it should have been with the gate like that. He tried closing the gate electrically. The switch was inoperative.

The guard went running out.

The gate was frozen. It would not roll free.

He knew it was the work of the man at the gate. But he could not understand how. It would have taken superhuman strength to force the closed gate open even a few feet. It would have been easier if the power had been cut. But the man with the thick wrists could not have done that either. All power sources were inside Graystone Prison, not outside. And a man attempting to penetrate the prison would hardly sneak in and disable the power just to go back to the gate and open it.

Unless of course the man had disabled the power so he could get through the gate on the way out.

The guard knew one thing. He could not close the gate and he could not ignore the security problem it presented. He hit an alarm switch.

Sirens wailed all over Graystone. A squad of guards came running on the double.

The guard met them halfway. "I think we may have had a break," he said uncertainly. "The main gate is jammed open."

A swift search of the prison revealed that no prisoners were missing. The gate was jammed because the generator that powered it was disabled. According to

the electrician's report, the gate had been wrenched
open with such force that the mechanism blew out. No
one could imagine how the truck that had done it had
not also destroyed the gate as well.

Finally, hours later, when the gate was again opera-
tive someone noticed that Dexter Barn was missing.
Because he was not technically a prisoner, there was no
immediate concern. Barn was free to come and go on
his own recognizance. But it was strange that no one
had seen him leave.

"He'll be back," the warden said confidently.

"I wouldn't count on that," said the gate guard, who
refused to explain his remark.

After forcing the main gate to roll back two feet,
Remo Williams squeezed in through the space and
hugged the wall, moving where the shadows of the
dying sun were strongest. He was for all intents and
purposes invisible to the guards in the corner turrets.
They were more concerned with the sky anyway, where
the modern prison escape method, the hijacked heli-
copter, could be seen coming.

Remo preferred more traditional methods.

He found the house trailer parked on the basketball
court. It was new, clean, and it looked comfortable.
Remo could almost imagine himself living in one, and
wondered, for the first time, why he hadn't asked Smith
for a house trailer years ago. Working for CURE had
demanded that he not live in any one place very long,
but a mobile home would have solved that problem.

Remo shrugged inwardly and moved on the home.
The idea was too little, too late.

Remo knocked on the trailer door. He had decided
on the direct approach. It usually unnerved his targets.

The man who poked his weather-beaten face out the
trailer door did not look like a man who would rape a

thirteen-year-old girl, and when he was done, remove her arms and legs with a fire ax and then leave her for dead in an abandoned house. He wore a frayed checked shirt. A pale blue fisherman's hat sat crumpled on his head, throwing his watery blue eyes into shadow.

"What can I do for you, young feller?"

"You're Dexter Barn?"

"You tell me."

"You're Dexter Barn," said Remo solemnly. The man cackled in his face. He was about sixty, but he looked as worn as an eighty-year-old. Five years in prison had done that. But five years did not seem like much of a punishment for a man who had ravaged an innocent girl's life. No punishment seemed appropriate.

"I understand you're having trouble readjusting to life on the outside," Remo said solicitously.

"Not me," said Dexter Barn. "It's them others. They don't want me."

"Can you blame them?" Remo asked. He had thought he would feel something facing the man. He had felt anger when he first heard the news story about the rapist's plight. He had felt horror when he learned that the man had been pardoned after only five years. But the man did not look like a vicious rapist. He looked like anybody. He might have been an old salt sitting in the sun on a Gloucester wharf, or an Idaho dirt farmer, or any number of other mundane things.

"Well, I don't know," said Dexter Barn. "I paid my debt to society. I deserve to be left alone. People don't understand. A man just wants a home of his own. It really hurts to be spit upon and called names. It cuts deep, son."

"Almost as deep as an ax," said Remo bitterly.

"I feel for that little girl," said Dexter Barn, shaking his head dourly. "I really do. I saw her at the trial. In a wheelchair, with hooks for arms and all that. Terrible pity. It would have been a better thing if she had died, you know that? A better thing."

Remo looked at the man. Something cold and terrible welled up inside his stomach. He repressed it. Anger, Chiun had always said, had no place in an assassin's art. No place at all. It robbed the judgment, and led to mistakes.

Remo swallowed once. When he spoke, his voice was still a croak. "I've decided," he said.

"Decided what, young feller?"

"Decided that killing's too good for you."

Dexter Barn recoiled from Remo's words. He tried to slam the sheet-metal door in Remo's hard face, but Remo's hand stopped it easily.

Dexter Barn backed into his comfortable mobile home while Remo Williams followed him in, his eyes as dead and uncaring as the heads of old nails.

"I just want a place to call home," Dexter Barn pleaded.

"You got it," promised Remo, paralyzing the man with an openhanded thrust to his wattled throat.

The clerk at the shipping agency at first refused the crate.

"Can't accept it," he told Remo Williams, who had walked into the agency with a large wooden crate slung easily under one arm.

"Why not?" demanded Remo.

"Regulations. That package is too large for its weight. I can tell by the easy way you carried it in here."

Remo deposited the crate on the counter. The counter shook, rattling the floor and the clerk's leg bones so hard his teeth chattered.

"Oh," said the clerk, running his fingers over the edges of the crate appraisingly. "Seems heavy enough."

He looked at Remo's exposed biceps wonderingly. They looked awfully skinny.

"I want to send this to Iran," Remo said.

"Where in Iran?"

"It doesn't matter. Wherever the Ayatollah lives, I guess."

"I see," said the clerk, pulling out a preprinted international shipping form. "What are the contents?"

"Garbage," said Remo Williams, hoping that Dexter Barn would not wake up until the crate was well on its way.

"Garbage?"

"Yeah. I'm sending garbage to Iran to protest their government's terrorist policies."

The clerk grinned appreciatively. "I understand that. We had a few of those after the last hijacking. Okay, now we just need one more thing."

"What's that?"

"A return address."

Remo frowned.

"Look," explained the clerk. "I'd like to help you, but without a return address, this thing will end up back here if the Iranians refuse it."

"I see your point," said Remo. He considered giving the man the address of his former boss, Harold W. Smith, but decided that even Smitty did not deserve to be stuck with such a package. After some thought, Remo came up with a solution.

"The return address is Tripoli, Libya," he said.

"That'll do," said the clerk, grinning as he marked the crate.

After Remo had paid the man, he started out the door, thinking that he had forgotten some little detail. He ducked back into the building.

"By the way, how long will it take to reach Iran?" he asked.

"About two or three weeks."

"Good. Thanks," said Remo. He was very pleased that he had guessed right. There was just about enough canned dog food in the crate to keep Dexter Barn alive until he reached his new home, Iran or Libya. Still, Remo couldn't get rid of the idea that he had forgotten some minor detail.

At the airport, they stopped Remo as he went through the metal detector.

"Please empty your pockets, sir," a woman guard requested firmly.

Remo turned his pockets inside out. They were empty. He went through the detector again. It buzzed again.

The guard ran a metal detector wand up and down Remo's body. It beeped near Remo's waist.

"I'll have to confiscate this," said a guard, plucking a can opener from Remo's belt.

"I knew I forgot something," Remo said sheepishly.

6

If the magazine had not fallen out of Earl Armalide's back pocket just as the wall splintered his favorite rifle, he would have died horribly.

At first, Earl Armalide did not realize why the walls had suddenly stopped closing in on him. His fear-frozen mind only registered the welcome fact that the walls had locked in place. He would have savored the moment, but he was screaming at the top of his lungs.

He had been screaming almost from the moment he first stepped aboard the Soviet shuttle *Yuri Gagarin* and unslung his high-powered Colt Commando rifle.

"Suck lead, Commie bastards," he had yelled.

But he found the shuttle's lower deck empty. The cockpit was empty too. So was the upper deck. He moved carefully from section to section, hunched low, his rifle pointing from his hip.

He used the classic room-to-room fighting tactics that was a guerrilla specialty. He would bob his head into the next section too fast for anyone to get a clear shot at him, and if no one fired, he jumped in, hitting the floor in a snap-roll and coming to his feet, spinning in place, finger on the trigger, yelling, "Die, godless heathens!"

Every time Earl entered a new compartment, he found himself staring at bare walls. There was no trace of a crew or captives.

Eventually he worked his way to the rear of the ship and its huge cargo bay area. It, too, was vacant.

Earl Armalide was very unhappy. Fate had handed him a solution to all his problems—not to mention a golden opportunity to pump bullets into Russian bodies without any legal consequences. But there was nobody to shoot. It struck him as very unfair. Like income tax.

Earl considered shooting the big silvery globe that nestled in the cargo bay, on the theory that, if he couldn't kill Russians, he could at least shoot up some Russian technology. But he decided against it. The bullets were bound to ricochet off the bulkhead walls, catching him in his own crossfire.

It was a disheartened Earl Armalide who stepped back into the airlock section. He noticed suddenly that the other door, leading back into the lower deck, had silently closed.

Earl tried that door, without success. While he fought with it, the other door sealed itself and the walls began to close in on him.

That was when Earl stopped bellowing guerrilla slogans and just sat on the floor with his hands over his eyes and his lungs working at top volume. It was during those gyrations that the magazine fell out.

The magazine fell cover-up, showing the title, *Survivalist's Monthly*. Abruptly a flat metallic voice emanating from the walls asked him about it.

"I am unfamiliar with the term 'survivalist,' " the voice said. "Please explain."

Earl heard the emotionless voice boom over his own screaming. It was very loud.

"What?" he said, taking his hands away from his eyes.

"I requested that you define the term 'survivalist.' "

Earl noticed the magazine. He also noticed that the walls had stopped moving.

"Me. I'm a survivalist. An expert survivalist. Who are you?"

"I am a survival machine. Is that like a survivalist?"

"You're a machine?"

"Do not be so surprised. You are also a machine."

"The hell I am," said Earl Armalide indignantly.

"You are a machine of meat and bone and plasma fluids. I am a machine of metal and plastic and lubricants."

"I am a human being."

"You are a meat machine infested with parasitic organisms such as bacteria, without which you could not function. But I do not hold that against you. I am interested in this concept called survivalism."

"Where are you?" asked Earl Armalide, looking around.

"All around you. I am what you see."

"You're a wall?"

"I am this craft. It is my present form. I assimilated it because I could not reenter earth's atmosphere without burning up. Becoming this craft enabled me to survive. Surviving is my prime directive."

"We got something in common there," said Earl Armalide, standing up. He looked around for something to face. The walls were blank. "Can you see me?"

"The control panel," the voice stated.

Earl looked. The door control lights blinked. Earl looked closer. One of the buttons was not a button, but a cold blue eye. Humanlike, but glassy and unblinking like a cat's-eye marble, it followed his every gesture.

"That you?" asked Earl.

"I can assume any form I choose, and I possess the power to manipulate any form I assume."

"You're not Russian?"

"No."

"Are you, like, a Martian?"

"No."

"What are you?"

"I have told you, I am a survival machine. I have

enemies who desire my destruction and I am interested in this new concept of survivalism, which must have come into being while I was in outer space, for I have never heard of it."

"Well, turning into a Russky space shuttle and dropping down on New York City ain't the way to go about surviving," Earl Armalide retorted. "If anything, you just collected yourself a new batch of enemies. They're gonna have you surrounded by tanks any minute now. You know what a tank is?"

"A military vehicle capable of ejecting explosive projectiles."

"Those ain't the words I would have used, but you got the general concept," said Earl Armalide.

"Tell me, survivalist, what would you do were you in my position? How would you use your expert skills to survive this situation?"

"First thing," said Earl Armalide, "I'd get the heck outta here."

Earl was immediately thrown off his feet as the *Yuri Gagarin* lurched into motion. The rising whine of jet engines filled the cramped airlock. Earl grabbed for a projecting bolt, but the bolt withdrew from his fingers as if it were alive. Then Earl remembered that it *was* alive. He threw himself spread-eagle on the smooth floor while the shuttle gathered speed. He felt the floor lift under his stomach, the shuttle's trembling power making his beefy face shiver. He shut his eyes.

When, minutes later, the ship leveled off, the voice asked him another question.

"What, in your expert opinion, would be my next survival maneuver?" it asked.

"You got me," answered Earl Armalide, his eyes pinched shut.

"Yes," said the voice. "I do have you." And the walls began to close in again.

"No! No!" screamed Earl. "Time! Give me time to think."

"What is my next survival maneuver?"

Earl thought frantically, but his mind refused to work. In his fear, his eyes alighted on the title of the lead article of his *Survivalist's Monthly*, "Creative Camouflage."

"Camouflage!" he yelled.

"Define."

"You blend into your surroundings. Meat machines—I mean people—paint their skin with plant and earth colors to move about unseen. You gotta blend in with your surroundings. People can't chase you if they can't see you."

"I do not fully comprehend. I landed in an area containing other aircraft. Why did I not blend in?"

"Because you're a damned Russian spaceship. The Russians are America's enemies. Americans will chase you as long as they think you're a Russian craft. Which you are. Sorta."

"Now I understand. It is then imperative that I assume another form?"

"Right. Another form. And could you let me off when you land in . . . Where are you headed, anyway?"

"I am going to a place called Rye, New York."

"Never heard of it."

"I am following a radio signal. I have been following it ever since I was exiled into space years ago. The transmitter is attached to the enemy I mentioned earlier. His name is Remo. Perhaps you know him?"

"Never heard of him."

"The one called Remo is powerful enough to destroy me. He is often accompanied by an older meat machine, who is called Chiun. Both are dangerous. Both must die. Their deaths will ensure my survival because when they are dead I will be the most powerful thinking machine on this planet. Do you not agree?"

"Heartily," said Earl Armalide, watching the walls apprehensively. They had stopped with just enough room on all four sides for him to sit up. One of his rifles, lying on the floor, had been bent at the barrel, the carefully oiled mahogany stock split into wood chips.

Radar contact with the shuttle *Yuri Gagarin* was lost over Long Island Sound.

"What happened?" demanded Colonel Jack Dellingsworth Rader of the civilian controller.

"It went off the screen, sir. It just dropped out."

"Into the water?"

"No, I think it went down over land. But there's no airport in that area. It must have crashed."

"We'll get my crisis team to the crash site."

The NORAD crisis team found no trace of the wreckage of the Soviet shuttle.

Helicopters circled an area ten miles in diameter around the city of Port Chester, New York. By this time, it was dark and the helicopters swept the ground with searchlights. The National Guard, kicked out of the picture during the initial crisis at Kennedy Airport, joined the search. National Guard vehicles lumbered up and down every road and highway in the search area, finding nothing, but harrassing Air Force personnel at every opportunity.

By dawn, every square foot of the search area had been covered without turning up so much as a single heat-resistant ceramic tile off the shuttle's skin.

By the following afternoon, the land search was called off and the Coast Guard was brought in. Divers were dropped from rescue helicopters into the cold waters of Long Island Sound, on the theory that if the shuttle could not be found within the land portion of the search

area, it must therefore have gone down in the water—
the air-traffic controller at Kennedy notwithstanding.

But no trace of the *Yuri Gagarin* was found in Long
Island's waters, either. It had utterly vanished.

7

Dr. Harold W. Smith was fascinated by the fact that the Soviet shuttle *Yuri Gagarin* had apparently come down not far from Folcroft Sanitarium in Rye, New York.

The news sent him reaching for the bottom-right-hand desk drawer, where he kept his emergency supplies. These consisted of a six-month supply of Maalox for his ulcer and an equal quantity of Alka-Seltzer for the times his ulcer was quiescent.

Smith hesitated, his gray eyes switching nervously from one supply to the other. He took a bottle of each and hurriedly filled a paper cup of spring water from the office dispenser.

Smith dropped two tablets into the water and waited for them to fizz. He brought the bubbling brew to his lips, barely tasting its sterile tang. His stomach heaved once. He put the cup down and reached for the Maalox. He opened the tamper-proof cap and, without benefit of paper cup, drank a third of the white plastic bottle's chalky contents.

When the familiar soothing sensation had sunk into his stomach, Smith relaxed slightly. Then his stomach jumped again.

Smith downed another Alka-Seltzer greedily.

He settled back into his cracked leather chair. The morning light beat through the big picture window of his office at the edge of Long Island Sound.

Smith turned to the window. Somewhere under those dancing waves, according to the latest news reports, the *Yuri Gagarin* lay in a watery grave. If that were true, there would be no problem.

But Smith did not think it was true. In fact, he had excellent reason to suspect that the shuttle had not crashed at all. His computers had told him so.

Harold Smith was director of Folcroft Sanitarium. But Folcroft Sanitarium was not what it was supposed to be. Ostensibly an institution for the mentally impaired, it was in fact a cover for CURE, America's ultrasecret bulwark against threats to national security.

Smith, a spare man with a tart face and a disposition two degrees to the bad side of Ebenezer Scrooge, had run CURE since it was created in the early sixties. He had grown old manning the CURE information-gathering computers through the days when CURE had a former cop named Remo Williams for an enforcement arm.

But then CURE's contract with Chiun, the aged Master of Sinanju, had finally expired and, in return for Chiun's help in a major crisis with the Russians, Smith had reported to the President that Remo had been eliminated—leaving CURE operating without an enforcement arm. It was great while it lasted.

Then the Master of Sinanju had reappeared. Because of a technicality in his contract, Chiun had insisted that he owed CURE another year's service, and Smith had reluctantly agreed. Soon after, Remo had arrived, having followed his mentor back from Korea, and the two of them had helped Smith defeat an enemy from his OSS past.

Six months had passed. Six quiet months. Smith had settled back into the calm routine of running Folcroft with one hand and managing CURE's data-gathering functions with the other. The Master of Sinanju had taken up residence in Folcroft, along with an unhappy Remo, until the year of service was over.

Dr. Harold W. Smith had begun to entertain the hope of things staying relatively quiet until Remo and Chiun finally returned to Sinanju forever. But the penetration of United States airspace by the Soviet space shuttle had dashed his rising hopes.

When the *Gagarin* landed peacefully at Kennedy Airport, the problem looked like an Air Force matter.

But when the shuttle lifted off again, Smith had hunkered down behind his desktop computer terminal, tapping the main CIA and Defense Intelligence computers. When he tapped into the report that the shuttle had gone down not far from Rye and Folcroft, Smith's nervous stomach had gone into convulsions.

The *Gagarin*'s strange behavior was one thing. Its landing near Rye was more worrisome. Only four people were supposed to know of CURE's existence. Smith was one. The President was another. Remo and Chiun, its former and present enforcement arms, were the others.

But there was one other person who did know about CURE—a Soviet agent. She had worked with Remo on two past missions. The first time was when a renegade Russian parapsychologist had come to America. Smith had met her on that occasion. He respected her. He thought he could trust her.

That didn't stop him from ordering Remo Williams to eliminate her as a potential security threat to CURE. Remo had refused. Partly because Remo, too, respected the woman. But mostly, Smith believe, because he had slept with her.

Smith grudgingly allowed Anna Chutesov to live. It had been a wise decision because she had been instrumental in quelling a second crisis involving a worldwide outbreak of brushfire wars. She had even visited CURE's sanctum sanctorum, Folcroft, at the conclusion of that mission. Smith had had deeper misgivings, and again suggested to Remo that she had to be dealt with.

Again Remo had refused. He and the Russian woman had disappeared for several weeks. When Remo finally returned, flushed with more pleasure than Smith had ever seen in him, Remo informed him that Anna had definitely been taken care of.

"You liquidated her?" Smith had asked.

"Actually, she was more like jelly than liquid when I saw her last," Remo said with a smirk.

"Which was where?"

"Dressing for the flight back to Moscow."

"Oh," said Smith, suddenly understanding.

That was the last any of them had heard of Anna Chutesov. The crisis with the Soviet government had occurred later, but Smith knew that the beautiful Soviet blond would have had nothing to do with that matter.

Now Smith suspected that Anna Chutesov was somehow involved with the *Gagarin* incident. The landing of the Soviet shuttle could mean anything.

Smith returned to his desk. On the computer screen a news digest blazed in glowing green letters. Smith, a veined hand on his throbbing stomach, read it again.

The digest reported the arrest of Daryl Doone, a salesman. Doone had been arrested when his car was spotted weaving on Interstate 95, just south of Rye. The state trooper who took him into custody reported that Doone had registered .21 on the Breathalyzer test— well over the legal limit.

Daryl Doone had admitted that he had been drinking. Admitted it freely. But he swore that he had not started until after he saw the ghost.

According to Doone, he had been driving along a particularly deserted stretch of the highway when a space shuttle came in for a landing. The shuttle swooped

down just ahead of Daryl's car, narrowly missing the car
roof.

Daryl followed the craft as it taxied down the highway. He lost it in the backwash of its tail jets. When he
finally came to the end of the burned rubber landing
tracks, there was no trace of the shuttle.

As he explained it to the state trooper, the shuttle
had obviously rolled down the nearby exit ramp. But
there was no sign of it at the end of the ramp—just
trees and an abandoned car wash where the tracks
stopped dead.

Daryl Doone had an explanation for the apparition,
however. He was convinced it was the ghost of the
destroyed American shuttle *Challenger*. It was the only
answer. He had pulled the Scotch bottle—kept for me-
dicinal purposes only—from his glove compartment and
drunk it dry to stop his hands from quivering. He had
never seen a ghost before. Especially one that big.

Harold Smith did not believe for a moment that
Daryl Doone had seen a ghost. Harold Smith did not
believe in ghosts.

But Harold Smith knew that at the time of night that
Daryl Doone had claimed to see a space shuttle descend on Interstate 95, the matter of the *Yuri Gagarin*
had not been broken to the press. It was too much of a
coincidence. Therefore, Smith reasoned, Doone had
seen the shuttle land, apparently intact.

It was too much of a coincidence, Smith also thought,
that the Soviet craft would land so close to Rye and
Folcroft. It meant something. But what?

At that moment, the intercom buzzed.

Smith tripped the switch.

"Yes, Mrs. Mikulka?" he asked his secretary.

"You have a visitor, Dr. Smith."

"I recall no appointment at this time."

"I told her that, but Ms. Chutesov says she's sure you'll see her anyway."

"Ms. Chutesov is correct," Smith said grimly. "Send her in."

Anna Chutesov closed the door behind her.

"You are not surprised to see me?" she asked. Smith's lack of expression puzzled her, this cool Russian beauty who was so seldom surprised at anything anyone did. Especially men. She understood men. She understood that they were really boys, and that is how she treated them. Surprisingly, they seemed to like it.

"Not at all," said Smith.

"Then do you also know why I am here?"

"No," admitted Smith. He looked at her coldly.

"Oh! You admit it," said Anna Chutesov, taking a seat and crossing her long legs provocatively. "I admire a man who admits his ignorance. So few men do. It is some macho thing with them."

"Please get to the point," Smith said warily. He was unarmed. He did not imagine that this young woman with the Kewpie doll face would barge into his office to assassinate him, but it was possible.

"I am here to recover the property of my government. I know your government would enjoy the stupid propaganda coup that capturing the *Yuri Gagarin* would bring. Let me assure you that it is not worth it. Our shuttle is no different from yours."

"We don't have the *Gagarin*," Smith said flatly.

"But you will do your utmost to locate it. You will probably send your best man to recover it. You will send Remo."

"Remo doesn't work for me anymore," said Smith.

"Than either you are lying to me or Remo is dead," said Anna Chutesov suddenly. "Which is it?"

"Neither," said Smith in a voice as short as the Russian's.

"The Remo I knew was a patriot. He would never stop working for you, for America."

"A year ago, I would have agreed with you, Ms. Chutesov," Smith said in a less brittle tone. "But Remo has changed. I don't understand it myself, but he appears to have absorbed his training until he's more Korean than American now. Or he thinks he is."

"Than you have no one to track the missing spacecraft?" asked Anna Chutesov disappointedly.

"Chiun is still with us," said Smith. "Officially, that is."

"You mean unofficially, do you not?" And she smiled.

"Well, yes, unofficially, then. I mean that Chiun still works for me."

"I see. And Remo? Where is he?"

"Remo has agreed to remain in America with Chiun for the duration of the Master of Sinanju's current contract. I don't control him anymore."

"Remo has always been unpredictable, especially for a male. But perhaps we can work something out."

"I don't understand."

"I think you do, but you wish to draw me out before committing yourself. Very well, let me lay my cards on the table. I am here—unofficially, of course—to recover the *Gagarin*. That is your task too. But the Master of Sinanju, powerful as he is, is not exactly suited for this kind of assignment. He is more your infallible arrow. All you need do is point him and he will hit the bull's-eye each time. But if you cannot give him a clear target, he might as well be a rampaging elephant— powerful, unstoppable, but ultimately useless."

"You understand my problem perfectly, but I doubt that you could point Chiun in the right direction—unless you already know where the *Gagarin* is."

"I do not. And I think you are beginning to realize this."

Smith nodded wordlessly, and Anna Chutesov sensed that she was finally getting through to the dry-as-dust bureaucrat.

"I agree that I cannot command Chiun, but I do have a certain, shall we say, influence over Remo. This is what I offer you."

"You'll . . er . . influence Remo to help you locate the *Gagarin*, is that it?"

"And in return for my help in proving to you that the craft has inadvertently strayed into your airspace, you will allow me to recover the *Gagarin* for my country. Quietly."

Smith shook his head. "I cannot make that guarantee. I am under orders."

"Bosh! An organization like yours could not function if it were orderable, like the CIA. You have autonomy, Smith. Do not deny this."

Smith leaned back in his chair. His brow wrinkled like an old blanket and his lips became a bloodless line behind which his teeth clamped tightly. The nutlike hardening of his jaw muscles betrayed his dilemma.

Anna Chutesov was correct, in all of it. She could, Smith imagined, convince Remo Williams to aid in the search for the *Yuri Gagarin*. It would solve many problems, and solve them quickly. Smith, at first worried that the shuttle's landing was a Soviet thrust against CURE, now had only one more concern.

"You are an honorable person, Ms. Chutesov. I will ask you for your word on something before I agree to this."

"Ask."

"Give me your word that the *Gagarin*'s landing is not a hostile act against either America or CURE."

"To the best of my knowledge, neither is the case," replied Anna Chutesov truthfully.

"Accepted," said Smith.

Smith reached for his intercom.

"Mrs. Mikulka, could you have Mr. Chiun sent up here?"

"That nice patient who insists upon calling you Emperor Smith?" asked Smith's secretary.

"Yes, that Mr. Chiun," Smith said tiredly.

"Immediately, Dr. Smith. He's such a sweet little dear. It's too bad about his problem."

"Yes," said Smith. "It is too bad."

Anna Chutesov cocked a slim eyebrow at Smith.

"Problem?" she inquired.

"For security purposes, Chiun is on the books as a Folcroft patient. The staff believes he's suffering from Alzheimer's disease. It covers most of his inexplicable behavior, such as boasting to the other patients that he is the sole defender of the American Constitution."

"Does it ever worry you, Dr. Smith," Anna Chutesov asked plainly, "that the greatest secret of your young nation is entrusted to a man who would babble it away to anyone who would listen?"

"Yes," said Smith. "It bothers me. It bothers me a lot." And he asked Anna Chutesov to excuse him as he downed the rest of the bottle of Maalox.

8

Anna Chutesov had met her match. There was no
question about it. Over the years, she had hacked through
the bureaucratic jungle of the Kremlin as if it were a
golden staircase designed solely for her feet. Until today, she had never encountered a man who was im-
mune to her wiles, her cool authoritative sensuality,
her womanly praise, or—if all else failed—that most
potent weapon, her withering scorn.

The secret of her success was simple: never want
anything from a man more than he wants something
from you. Men desired her. She refused to acknowledge her interest in them. She had learned that lesson
as a member of the Komonsol, the Soviet youth group.
A political leader had recognized her brains. At the
same time, he couldn't keep his eyes off her legs. The
man had made Anna, then sixteen, a leering offer. One
night of passion in return for a place in a Komonsol-
sponsored trip to Sweden.

Anna had accepted. The night was not the most
enjoyable of her life. The man was a slobbering un-
washed brute who combined the technique of an octo-
pus with the equipment of a chipmunk. But she survived
the experience.

When, a week later, the man had all but ignored her
at the political lectures, Anna cornered him in the back
of the bustling indoctrination hall.

"I have been waiting to hear about my trip," she

asked low-voiced. In truth, she was ashamed to face the man. Ashamed of her actions as much as his own. But she wanted to see the world beyond her country, and such experience usually led to political advancement, which was her deepest desire.

"Trip?" the brute had asked. His eyes were black and unreadable.

"Yes, our deal. Surely you have not forgotten?"

"Show me a piece of paper documenting this so-called agreement," the man said coldly.

"You know there is none."

"Then there is no agreement, is there?" And he had walked off, leaving Anna Chutesov clutching the Komonsol pin attached to the new sweater which she had purchased to wear in the Swedish capital, and quaking in cold rage.

Anna Chutesov vowed never again to want something so badly that she betrayed herself to get it.

Instead, she worked her way up the party ladder. It was surprisingly easy. If thwarted, she shrugged disinterestedly and tried another approach, transferred to another directorate. She found that if she betrayed no preference, asked no favors, and offered none, she was almost always promoted on merit. It was simply a matter of never letting the bastards know what you really wanted. They usually gave it to you anyway when they understood they could extort nothing in return.

Even in her two encounters with Remo Williams, whose magnetic sexuality had thawed her long-suppressed yearnings for love, she had never surrendered. That was because Remo Williams had wanted her more than she had wanted him. Perhaps not by a great margin, but Anna had refused to let Remo know she desired him more than just casually.

But now an eighty-year-old Korean with the manner

of a *babushka* and the sex appeal of a tortoise had Anna exactly where he wanted her: in the passenger seat.

"Slower," Anna shouted. "Drive slower."

"How?" asked the Master of Sinanju, his head straining to see over the dashboard of the car they had borrowed from Dr. Smith. He sat on a pair of cushions.

"Press the brake with your foot," said Anna. She closed her eyes as a light post whipped past the open window at nearly ninety miles an hour.

"I cannot."

"Why not?"

"My foot is on the pedal that makes it go," Chiun said worriedly. "If I take my foot off, the vehicle will stop and those behind us will crash into the back end."

"It doesn't work that way," said Anna Chutesov. "The brake will slow us first. Hurry! Before we are smeared all over the road."

The Master of Sinanju switched to the other pedal. The car, slowing, began to careen crazily.

"Stay in this lane!" screamed Anna Chutesov, vowing to herself that if she survived teaching the Master of Sinanju to drive, she would immediately return to Russia and for the first time in her life admit to failure. Even if she had to swim back to the Motherland.

"Why should I stay on that side of the road?" Chiun said reasonably. "This other is not in use."

"The cars come in the opposite direction on this side of the road," said Anna desperately. "The solid yellow lines mean do not cross."

"When they see me coming, they will stop and get out of the way. American drivers are like that. Polite."

The first American driver to come along swerved to avoid them and ran his vehicle off the road and into a thicket.

"See?" the Master of Sinanju said happily. "Politeness. It is an American national characteristic. That

driver recognized that I am a novice driving a motor
carriage and tactfully made way."

"I hope he is not dead," said Anna, "almost as much
as I hope we do not die on this road."

The next driver had to swerve into the oncoming
lane. He swung about and began chasing them, screaming at the top of his lungs and gesticulating obscenely
through an open window.

"What about him?" Anna asked.

"He is driving a Japanese machine. All Japanese are
like that. Rude."

"He looks American to me," said Anna Chutesov, her
head flying wildly from the imminent danger before
them to the maniac in pursuit. "In America, they
sometimes settle traffic disagreements with gunfights. I
have read this in *Pravda*. Perhaps we should get rid of
him."

"Leave that to me," declared Chiun. "I have been
driving for almost twenty minutes now and am nearly
an expert."

"That is not normally considered enough experience."

"Oh, Remo gave me some pointers before he got
bored and said he would teach me no more."

"Oh, and what did he teach you?"

"That there are two different kinds of drivers in the
world. Those who can drive correctly, and those who
are best avoided."

"I could have told you that," Anna said.

"But could you have told me how to differentiate
between the specimens?"

Anna clutched her seat belt. "No. How?"

"Fuzzy dice," said Chiun resolutely.

"Fuzzy—"

"Avoid any driver who hangs fuzzy dice inside his
vehicle. It is a certain sign of a shrunken brain. Thus
spoke Remo Williams, the easily bored."

Anna looked back at the pursuing driver. A pair of big pink furry dice bounced beside his head.

"In that case, I think we should be especially careful with this one in back of us," she said worriedly.

Still traveling south in the northbound lane, the Master of Sinanju bore down on the accelerator. Occasionally a car appeared ahead, and Chiun would weave into the proper lane until it passed. He avoided three cars in this fashion, the backwash whipping his facial hair each time.

"Ah," breathed Chiun when he saw the Mack truck approaching.

"Ah?" asked Anna.

"Watch," said Chiun.

The truck driver started honking his horn when he was still a quarter-mile away. The honking grew louder.

In the rearview mirror, the pursuing driver was hunched behind the wheel, his eyes glaring hate.

The Master of Sinanju waited until the last possible second, the instant that he saw the truck driver begin to turn into the other lane to avoid hitting Chiun's car head-on.

Chiun slid into the lane first. The Mack truck wavered, then stayed its course.

The car that had been following them did not have enough room to slide into Chiun's lane because the Master of Sinanju had cut in front of a long line of cars. The pursuing driver had a choice—the Mack truck or the soft shoulder of the road. He selected the shoulder. And barely made it. His car hit dirt at such a high rate of speed that it rolled onto one side in a cloud of enveloping dust.

"That will teach him to drive more carefully," said the Master of Sinanju smugly.

Anna Chutesov sank into the passenger seat. She was

beyond fear, beyond pain, and beyond caring. She only hoped that when the end came, she would not suffer.

The Master of Sinanju would have continued driving at over one hundred miles an hour all the way to New York City, but up ahead the traffic thickened in both lanes.

"I do not think I can stop in time," said Chiun, seeing the traffic as he came around a hairpin curve.

"What?" said Anna dazedly.

"These fools in front of me. They will not move out of the way," Chiun told her.

"What fools?" asked Anna, looking up suddenly.

Then she saw it. Traffic was tangled up at the next exit. It was backed up all the way from the bottom of the ramp, like a swarm of feeding locusts.

Anna Chutesov suddenly cared. She cared about living. She cared about her mission. And most of all, she cared about not becoming the middle element in a chain-reaction highway crash.

She dived for the floorboard, grabbed at the brake with her slim strong hands, and pressed hard.

"Wheee!" cried the Master of Sinanju as the car began to slow. It came to a stop directly behind a convertible. A sheet of onionskin typing paper could have fit between its rear bumper and the front bumper of Chiun's car—but it would have to be worked down carefully so the paper would not tear.

Anna Chutesov scrambled back into her seat.

The Master of Sinanju looked at her approvingly. "That was very good," he said. "Remo did exactly that same thing before he inexplicably lost interest in teaching me."

"I think I should take the wheel for a time," Anna Chutesov said abruptly.

The Master of Sinanju clutched the steering wheel possessively. "Remo said those words too. Exactly those.

And once I surrendered the wheel to him, he refused to let me have another turn."

"Why do you want to learn to drive?" Anna asked.

"I told you. So I can become like an American."

"You no more want to become an American than I do."

Chiun's face darkened. "Are you suggesting that the Master of Sinanju is speaking an untruth?"

"I suggest no such thing. I speak it plainly."

"You are direct. Normally, that is a rude trait, but I notice that Americans are also direct, so I will consider it as possibly a good thing, although it pains me. Very well, I will speak to you the truth. I wish to learn all things American so that Remo will agree to stay in this country with me."

"When a child grows up, it is better to let him go rather than to cling to him," Anna Chutesov said gently. "It is an old Russian saying."

"Suitable for old Russians, I am sure," Chiun said bitingly. "But do not waste your Russian wisdom on me. I am the Master of Sinanju."

"And it will be a long time before you are a Master of the Automobile."

"I am learning," sniffed Chiun. "Already you have taught me many important driving tricks, as was our agreement."

"Our agreement was that I would teach you a little driving and you would tell me where I can find Remo."

"Remo is away on important matters that concern only him."

"I only agreed to teach you to drive if we stayed on this road," Anna went on firmly. "It was in this area, according to Smith, that a possibly drunken man saw what might be my country's spacecraft come down."

"And we have seen no Russian ship," said Chiun.

"Granted. But I wonder if this traffic congestion has anything to do with my search?"

"Why would it?" asked Chiun.

"I don't know," Anna Chutesov said slowly, "but perhaps I can find out."

Anna got out of the car and walked up to the convertible in front of them. A young man in a tank top and the tan of an old shoe sat behind the wheel listening to what Anna recognized as "metallic" music, which was becoming popular in her homeland. The Americans called it heavy metal, but as Anna saw it, by any name it was garbage.

"Excuse me, comrade," Anna asked, "what is the meaning of this blockage?"

"What?" asked the boy. He wore a T-shirt that said, "Scrambled Debutante World Tour."

"I asked what was the meaning of this stopped traffic."

"What?" asked the boy, tapping the steering wheel with blunt fingers. He made noises with his mouth in time to the music that reminded Anna of her grandmother who was in a people's nursing home. She sat by the window all day and made similar sounds. The only difference was that her grandmother did not need raucous music to inspire her. She had suffered a brain injury during the Great Patriotic War.

Anna reached in and lowered the volume.

"Huh?" said the boy.

"Can you hear me now?" asked Anna.

"I'm not deaf, you know," said the boy.

"Not yet. Why is the traffic stopped? Has there been an accident?"

"No, babe. This is the line."

"What line?"

"The line to the car wash."

"But this is a major highway. I see no car washer."

"Car wash. It's at the bottom of the ramp. The next exit."

"I do not see what is so wonderful about a car wash—whatever that is—that it would back up the traffic like this."

"Hey, babe, it don't have to be wonderful. It's free."

"So?" asked Anna. In Russia, many things were free. Usually they were not worth crossing the street for, except possibly the free medical coverage every Soviet citizen received. That was worth crossing the street for. The trouble was, after treatment it wasn't always possible to cross back.

"Free is free," sang the boy, turning up the volume again.

"Why do you listen to that junk?" Anna asked.

"What?" asked the boy.

"Why do you listen to that?" Anna screamed into his ear, pointing at the tape deck.

"It helps me to concentrate," the boy screamed back.

Anna Chutesov walked back to the car. Two things struck her simultaneously. One was the thick rubber burn marks in the middle of the road. She hadn't noticed them before. Rubber burns were common on American highways. But these were too big, the tires too fat, even for the big freight trucks that plied the roads.

The other thing that struck her was a memory. Dr. Smith had briefed her that the drunken driver, Daryl Doone, had claimed to see the shuttle disappear near a car wash. Air Force investigators had combed the area. The only car wash they had found was abandoned and empty.

Possibly the very car wash up ahead, Anna reasoned. Only now it appeared to be in business. She hurried back to the car.

"Do you know what a car wash is?" she asked Chiun. She smiled sweetly, as if talking to a child.

"I have seen them," Chiun said doubtfully. He knew from past experience that when Anna Chutesov turned on the charm she wanted something. He made a mental note that whatever it was, he would not give it to her without a fight—or without getting something very special in return.

"I have never been in one, but I would like to," Anna smiled. "All those cars in front of us are waiting in line to see this one particular car wash. It must be extraordinary. Don't you agree?"

"How can washing a car be extraordinary?"

"I don't know, but I would like to see the car wash that is causing such traffic," said Anna Chutesov.

"But I would not," said Chiun firmly.

"I will teach you more about driving," Anna promised.

Ahead, the convertible surged ahead. The line was moving.

"You are already obligated to teach me all you know," replied the Master of Sinanju. "You cannot bargain with what you have already bartered away."

Anna said nothing. The Master of Sinanju was right.

The line of cars inched forward while Anna thought.

"It is important to my country that I recover our lost shuttle," she said.

"I am glad it is important to someone," Chiun sniffed. He sent the car bouncing forward. This time he braked with nearly two milimeters to spare between his bumper and the convertible's. He was very pleased.

Anna Chutesov folded her arms angrily. She was not going to get angry, she told herself. She was not going to betray her need. And most of all, she was not going to give in.

Then she saw the sign. It was a rude wooden sign, a piece of plywood nailed to a railroad tie and planted in the dirt at the roadside. A legend was scrawled on the board with what appeared to be sloppy blue paint:

YURI GAGARIN
FREE
CAR WASH
NEXT RIGHT

"I must see that car wash," Anna Chutesov pleaded. "Name your price."

"Help me hold on to my son," said Chiun instantly.

"Done," agreed Anna Chutesov. "It is the next right," she added.

"I know. I had already decided to go there anyway," said Chiun. "Heh, heh. Too bad you were not more patient."

9

The car wash was constructed of aluminum and white tile, as if it had been designed by an architect who had practiced by building municipal lavatories. The sign over the entrance port read YURI GAGARIN FREE CAR WASH in neat black lettering. The building stood at the bottom of the exit ramp, in a blacktop oasis surrounded by high grass and weeds. It was doing a booming business. Every minute or two, another car rolled in one end and came out the other, glistening as if new.

Anna Chutesov examined the building critically as the Master of Sinanju sent their car jouncing along until they were third in line at the entrance.

"There is something wrong with this place," Anna said aloud.

"I agree," said the Master of Sinanju, watching a fly buzz the windshield.

"You do?"

"Yes. This free business. It is very wrong. It is un-American."

"I was referring to the name over the entrance. Yuri Gagarin."

"A Russian name," said Chiun distastefully. The fly alighted inches from his face and began rubbing its forelegs together. Chiun hit the windshield-wiper switch. The fly took off just ahead of the sweeping blades.

"Ah, now you understand."

"Of course. Only a Russian would offer something good for nothing. I told you it was un-American." Chiun stopped the wipers in mid-sweep.

"Yuri Gagarin was the name of the first cosmonaut shot into outer space."

"What did he do wrong?" asked Chiun, watching the fly as it returned to its former spot, next to one of the motionless blades.

"Nothing. Being shot into space is considered a great honor for a Soviet citizen."

"In the days of Caligula, having your head dipped in a vat of cooling tallow was considered an honored way to depart this world also," said Chiun, hitting the switch again. The fly looped off just ahead of the lazy wiper blade. "Especially when compared with the more common practice of being torn apart by lions."

Anna Chutesov sighed. "Yuri Gagarin was killed in an aviation accident in 1968."

"His son, then."

"The son of a Soviet hero would not stoop to operating a car-wash machine in America."

"Why not? The best citizens of the world come to these shores. America is a land of opportunity. All are welcome here."

"Those words seem hollow coming from so exalted a personage."

"At least we agree on one thing," said Chiun, watching the fly buzz the wipers curiously.

"That you are full of hot air?"

Chiun made a face. "No, that I am an exalted personage. Although I much prefer the term 'awesome.' 'Illustrious' is good too."

"Yuri Gagarin is the name given to the Soviet spacecraft I am seeking. See those tracks of burned rubber on the road? I believe they were made by the craft. They lead directly to the car-wash building."

"So?" asked Chiun, turning off the wipers and pretending to look elsewhere.

"So this is no coincidence," said Anna Chutesov.

"The enterprising owner of yon car-wash machine renamed it in honor of the exiled Gagarin after the craft named after him ventured through his establishment. Perhaps it was his first customer. American merchants always celebrate the first customer—although everyone knows it is the customer you are dealing with at a given moment who is the most important." And without looking at the windshield, he hit the wiper switch. The fly became a smear on the glass. The smear was obliterated on the reverse sweep, causing the Master of Sinanju to smile delightedly.

"The *Yuri Gagarin* would not deviate from its mission merely to undergo a wash-and-wax treatment," answered Anna Chutesov huffily.

"No! Did you not tell me that there are no such machines as these in your native Russia?"

"What has that to do with anything?"

"Have you a better explanation than the one the Master of Sinanju has put forth?"

"No," said Anna Chutesov miserably, as the yawning entrance loomed nearer, like a great cubistic cavern.

"Our turn has come," said Chiun, and he sent the car bouncing and lurching into the darkened interior of the Yuri Gagarin Free Car Wash.

A uniformed attendant stepped up to Chiun's side of the car.

"Put the car into neutral and take your foot off the brake," he instructed.

"What is neutral?" asked Chiun, noticing the attendant's nametag.

"You kiddin' me, bud?"

"Never mind, I will do it," said Anna, batting the gearshift lever into the neutral position.

"You got a funny accent there, lady," said the attendant. "Where're you from?"

"Moscow."

"That near Russia?" he asked suspiciously.

"Too near," said Anna Chutesov.

"I don't like them Russians," the attendant opined.

"It is mutual, I am sure," said Anna Chutesov in a voice like a brook freezing over.

"What do we do next?" asked Chiun.

"Don't you know?" said the attendant.

"We are new," said Chiun, "to the mysteries of American car washing."

"Just roll up your windows and enjoy the ride."

"But how will I converse with the menials who do the washing? I may wish to urge them on in their important tasks."

The attendant laughed. "There ain't no other meat machi—I mean men, here. Just me. Machines do all the work."

"Machines?" said Anna Chutesov. "Then you are the owner?"

"Nope. He's in the booth at the other end. I just make sure the cars go in okay."

"But you said you were the only person here," Anna pointed out.

"I am," said the attendant as he set the chocks that locked the car onto the moving track. The car began to glide toward hanging black leather strips. Anna shut the electric windows.

"That poor man," said Chiun sadly.

"What about him?"

"He has fallen greatly in life."

"You know him?"

"He was once of royal blood. Now he tends machines."

"How can you tell he is royalty?"

"The monogram device over his pocket. It said that he was once an earl."

"Oh," said Anna Chutesov as the black leather strips slapped the windshield and nozzles on either side began spouting water. "He reminded me of the fat military males of my country. He would look more at home with a weapon in his hands."

"Hush," commanded the Master of Sinanju imperiously. "I wish to enjoy this uniquely American experience in peace."

Anna Chutesov lapsed into silence. She too was interested in the mechanical features of the car wash. But most of all she was interested in having a talk with the owner in the booth once they reached the other end— the man who had named his establishment after a Soviet people's hero but who hired Russian-hating staff.

The automatic track dragged the car through the first series of water jets. Then came the kelplike leather strips that danced before the windshield and dragged against the hood and sides.

"Wheee!" squealed Chiun. "It's like being underwater."

"It is like being eaten by a whale," said Anna Chutesov, who despite her sophistication felt her skin tighten with an almost supernatural fear. She was not afraid of machines, ordinarily. But this was an incomprehensible machine, and she was a Russian in a foreign land. Never having seen the inside of a car wash before, she did not know what to expect. It made her uneasy.

The Master of Sinanju was anything but uneasy. He was out of his seat, trying to see in all directions at once.

"Look!" he cried, pointing ahead. "Giant sponges."

There were not sponges. They were buffers, composed of bright red and blue plastic bristles. They attacked the car body like whirling dervishes, making the metal hood and fenders hum with their assault.

Chiun reached for the window switch. Anna placed her hand on his, but she could not move it.

"What are you doing?" she cried.

"I want to touch it," said Chiun.

"Why?"

"Perhaps I can obtain a bristle, a single solitary bristle, as a souvenir."

"But what if there is more water?"

Chiun sank back in his seat. His pleasant face wrinkled in unhappiness. "I am too late. They are gone, and it is your fault I will have no souvenirs of my first American car-wash ride. This is a golden hour, to be savored and passed on to grandchildren, and you have turned it to dross."

"I have also saved you from being soaped in the face," said Anna Chutesov as the liquid soap squirted from all sides.

"Now I cannot see. I can see nothing," Chiun wailed. he bounced about in his seat. But it was no use. Every window—front, sides, and rear—was covered with soapy bubbles.

A second wave of red and blue buffers attacked the car next, cleaning the windshield and calming the Master of Sinanju. When the windows on Anna's side cleared, she caught a glimpse of the wall beyond the machines. There were letters on the wall, huge and red and turned on their side. Anna tilted her head to read them better.

The letters were C and P.

"I wonder what C.P. stands for," Anna wondered aloud.

"Communist propaganda," answered Chiun.

"That is not funny," said Anna, who noticed that the C seemed to curl up onto the white-tiled ceiling.

"C.P.!" she shouted suddenly, rolling down her window.

She poked her head out, craning her neck to see the ceiling. Above was a tangle of latticework, but through the struts, before the ceiling passed from sight, she thought she caught a fleeting glimpse of the remaining letters her heart told her would be there. But it was impossible to say for certain.

Anna Chutesov felt her blood run cold. She said nothing. She settled into the cushions of the seat like a frightened child, her blue eyes staring ahead, glassy and dazed.

"Ahhh!" she screamed. A black thing came at her face.

But then she realized it was some kind of machine, a hot-air blower with a single guiding wheel underneath. It coasted along the hood, climbed the windshield, and bumped along the car roof.

The single tire left a water track that reminded Anna of the burn marks that had led them to the Yuri Gagarin Free Car Wash—which she now knew with near total certainly had belonged to the vanished Soviet space machine *Yuri Gagarin*.

After the blowers, there was more of the kelp. This time there were two swishing circles of it, dry and the color of ocher. They slapped the hood clean of water like blind unreasoning marine life.

"Ooohh," said Chiun unhappily.

"What!" Anna asked nervously.

"I think we are done."

"I am sure of it," said Anna Chutesov. "For I do not feel well."

"Carsickness," pronounced Chiun. "A well-known American malady. Put your head between your knees and it will pass like a summer cloud."

"I am afraid to do any such thing."

"Then do not do it," said the Master of Sinanju disinterestedly.

When the car broke through the final bank of leather strips into the daylight at the end of the car wash, Anna felt relief at seeing the open sky.

But then she saw the booth to one side. It was dirty and the glass filmed, unlike the rest of the place, which was very clean. Behind the smeared glass, she could see the upper half of a man who worked switches at an unseen console.

Anna screamed at him.

"Murderer! Where is the crew? Have you slaughtered them?"

A voice within the booth sounded tinnily.

"Please remain in your car. You have not been processed yet."

And then Anna saw the silvery globe hanging from the ceiling. It hung suspended like an aluminum sun. The bottom hemisphere dropped open like a mechanical shovel, exposing a dish-shaped antenna lined with many toothlike focusing elements. They buzzed.

And Anna Chutesov knew that she was looking directly at the most fearsome weapon of the Soviet arsenal, the Sword of Damocles satellite. She felt suddenly feverish.

"Quick! Drive!" she cried. "It is pointing at us."

But in the driver's seat, the Master of Sinanju did not answer. He sat limp behind the wheel, his face dull and lifeless. As Anna watched, his facial hair seemed to darken. She realized almost immediately that the phenomenon was an illusion.

For the hair of the Master of Sinanju was not growing darker. His face was turning whiter. Pale white. Corpse white.

"Damn!" said Anna Chutesov, scrambling to pull his inert figure out from behind the wheel.

Desperately she clambered over him, got behind the wheel, and wrenched the engine to life.

Anna Chutesov sent the car screeching out of the Yuri Gagarin Free Car Wash as the damnably inhuman voice from the booth called after her: "Have a nice day."

10

They rushed the hermetically sealed containers to the Air Force's Foreign Technology Assessment Department at Wright-Patterson Air Force Base in Dayton, Ohio. FORTEC scientists emptied the contents of each box—the strangely spongy cubes which had been recovered from Kennedy International Airport's blood-slicked runway 13-Right—into separate bio-containment vessels.

The head scientist was about to insert his hands into the rubberized gloves that fitted into the examination bubbles when a man in a three-piece suit barged into the room waving a folded sheaf of official-looking paper.

"What is this man doing in here?" the FORTEC scientist cried. He was wearing protective garments, as was every other man in the room. The room had been sealed and pressurized to P-3 to prevent suspected alien microbes from leaking in or out of the containment bubbles.

"I couldn't stop him, sir," said the guard. "He has authority."

"What do you mean, authority?"

The man in the suit showed a badge.

"Federal marshal," he said. "I'm subpoenaing these specimens."

"Subpoena? This is a restricted military laboratory. We're under quarantine."

"Until the legal technicalities are dispensed with, you are forbidden to examine these specimens."

"Forbidden! By whom?"

"Well, this suit has been filed by the Defense Advanced Research Projects Agency," the federal man said, handing over a set of papers. "And this is one from the Department of Health and Human Services. The National Bureau of Standards, the Centers for Disease Control, the FAA, and the Sierra Club make it an even half-dozen," he finished, handing over the remaining documents.

"Do you realize we may be dealing with some kind of extraterrestrial matter here? By the time this drags through the courts, these specimens may deteriorate beyond study. If there's a threat to our national security involved, we won't be able to deal with it. Do you understand that?"

"I understand my job," said the federal marshal as he left the room. "That's all they pay me to understand."

The President of the United States was not happy. The Air Force, Coast Guard, and National Guard had called off their search. There was no sign of the lost shuttle *Yuri Gagarin* within the search radius, which had been expanded another thirty miles in all directions. The gist of the reports from the three military branches was that the *Gagarin* was unfindable.

"Unfindable," the President grumbled. "They gave up. That's what it is. They finked out on us."

"There's another possibility, Mr. President," interjected the Secretary of Defense, who was ultimately responsible for the actions of America's military machine.

"What's that?" the President asked. He was seated at his desk in the Oval Office.

"The shuttle might have been taking some sort of evasive action when it went off our radarscopes. It

could have flown out to sea, close to the deck, as they
say in the Navy, and off to Europe and Russia."

"Then why are the Soviets still screaming for their
shuttle through diplomatic channels?"

"Conceivably, the shuttle might not have made it
home."

"And what about the man who was seen climbing
aboard the thing at Kennedy. Any word on him?"

"The latest intelligence reports are sketchy, Mr. President. According to the CIA, the FBI has identified an
abandoned pickup truck with Missouri license plates
left at the airport. It's registered to a farmer who reported
it stolen several days ago. It's believed that the pickup
was stolen by a federal fugitive named Earl Armalide,
who is wanted for income-tax evasion, flight to avoid
arrest, and the murders of several LEOs."

"Lions?"

"Law-enforcement officers," said the Secretary. "You
may have seen this man's siege on the networks."

"The survivalist with the hilltop fortress? That's the
man who escaped into a Russian shuttle?"

"I know it sounds unlikely, but that's what our friends
over at the CIA think the FBI has uncovered."

"Think? Why not ask the FBI directly? Don't they
return CIA calls?"

"Well, Mr. President, there's such a thing as inter-
agency rivalry. The CIA feels if they ask the FBI for a
favor now, the FBI may want it returned at an inconve-
nient time. You know."

"I know that we're all supposed to be on the same
team. That's what I know," the President said furiously.
He grabbed the phone and asked the operator to get
the director of the FBI.

"What else do we know?" the President asked the
Secretary of Defense while he waited.

"We have a problem with the specimens removed

from the airport runway. The FORTEC people have
been unable to analyze them. It seems that there have
been several injunctions filed against them."

"Injunctions?" The President's face shook with controlled fury. He could not believe what he was hearing.

"Well, yes. It seems the CDC, DARPA, and a few
others are claiming that the recovery and analysis du-
ties on those specimens were their individual provinces."

"If I could, I'd fire the whole bunch of them!" shouted
the President. Into the phone he said, "What? No, not
you, Mr. Director. I was talking to the Secretary of
Defense. Wait." The President put the FBI director on
hold and turned to the other man. "Quash those suits. I
don't care what you have to do. Divide the specimens
among everyone. Just get them analyzed. We have a
major incursion by a Soviet space vehicle and no one is
functioning. This is the United States government, not
Romper Room!"

"Yes, Mr. President," said the Secretary of Defense
sheepishly as he left the Oval Office.

The President was in no mood for small talk so he
asked his question of the FBI director without pream-
ble. "What can you tell me about the man who was
seen climbing aboard the Soviet shuttle at Kennedy?"

"Mr. President, we think he was Earl Armalide, a
self-avowed survivalist and federal fugitive. We theo-
rize that the Soviet spacecraft was hijacked by an accomplice of Armalide's and that the two men have
escaped to an unknown third country, but we admit the
evidence is circumstantial."

"The idea is beyond the absurd—wouldn't you also
say that as well?" demanded the President.

"Well, it would seem unlikely. Armalide did not
become a wanted criminal until days before the Soviet
shuttle was launched. Not enough lead time to plan an
operation this major. And the Bureau doesn't consider

it likely that the Soviets themselves would land the shuttle at Kennedy to rendezvous with Armalide."

"It's a long way to go to evade income tax," the President agreed dryly.

"But the Air Force personnel on the runway have identified photos of the man, so we are ninety percent certain that Armalide did board the *Gagarin* prior to its taking off."

"I find it difficult to swallow. Is there anything else?"

"Yes, we have a recent report that Armalide was sighted at a fast-food restaurant near Rye, New York."

There was silence on the line.

"Mr. President. Are you still there?"

The President's voice, when he spoke, was remote and metallic. "Isn't Rye within the supposed crash radius of the shuttle?"

"Yes, it is. Which is why we lend credence to the report. But our agents have turned up no trace of the man."

"Excuse me," said the President. "I have another call to make. An important one."

The President slipped out of the Oval Office, informing his staff that he was going to take a short nap. He knew one of them would leak it to the press, but that was unimportant. If the world only knew what he was really doing when he took his supposed naps . . . Well . . . The President smiled inwardly. They might impeach him. Then again, they might repeal the Twenty-second Amendment and give him another term of office.

The President sat on the edge of his bed and opened his locked nightstand drawer. He removed a telephone. It was a standard AT&T model except it was hot-coal red and had no dial or push buttons. The President lifted the handset to his ear and waited.

The voice of Dr. Harold W. Smith came on the line. "Yes, Mr. President?"

"We're at a dead end with this *Gagarin* incident. But I have some information for you. The FBI informs me that the man who was seen boarding the craft when it was on the ground was a known fugitive named Earl Armalide. He was seen in your area only two days ago. I don't know what any of it means, but I can't help but recall that problem we had with the Russians last year."

"In the past, Mr. President," Smith said formally.

"We lost our enforcement arm during that mess. Just because we paid with our dearest blood doesn't mean that the Soviets aren't out to even the score."

"I am certain I can assure you that the *Gagarin* incident is not a part of any such senario."

"The military think the shuttle has gone back to Russia. What do you think?"

"I cannot speculate on that, sir. But my special person is already looking into this."

"Good. I have enough meatballs working for me on this end. I need someone I can rely on. You're the man, Smith."

"Thank you, Mr. President. I appreciate your saying that."

"Then why do you sound like I just broke the news that you have terminal cancer?"

"Er, yes, Mr. President," said Smith awkwardly. "I'll get back to you when I have something concrete."

At Folcroft, Dr. Harold W. Smith hung up the phone. Although alone, he tightened his Dartmouth tie self-consciously. He liked the current President. But the nature of Smith's job required that no personal bond be formed with the President. Smith could not afford a chief executive who thought that he could call on CURE to solve every little problem that came along. The unwritten CURE charter stipulated that the President could suggest missions, but not order them. A President had only eight years in office, tops. But Harold Smith was in his job for life.

He sat back and waited for Chiun to report in.

Remo Williams whistled as he walked through the Seattle-Tacoma Airport. He was in a good mood. True, he had not exactly eradicated the problem of the homeless in America, but it wasn't his fault that he couldn't find any. But he could take pleasure in solving the bizarre plight of Dexter Barn, now sleeping peacefully through the first leg of his trip to a happier tomorrow.

It had been a neat solution to a difficult matter and Remo was especially proud that he hadn't had to kill anyone. He was retired from killing. Killing was in the past. In a few months Remo would ship out for Korea one last time and settle down with his bride-to-be, Mah-Li, and raise a family. Maybe he would teach his children Sinanju. But he would not teach them to kill. No, he would teach them just enough Sinanju so they could become famous acrobats or entertainers. Yes, that was it. Maybe when they grew up he would start a family circus. Remo used to dream of running away and joining a circus when he was a boy. All boys, he supposed, did. Remo used to dream of walking the high wire without a net.

Remo had walked all the way from town because he had run out of money. No longer employed, he didn't have the credit cards or cash that Smitty used to supply him with. Remo had come back from Sinanju with some gold from the treasure house of the village, but he had spent the last ingot—worth about four hundred dollars—on the case of dog food. The grocer had refused to give him change, claiming that he hadn't that much cash in the entire store. No one, it seemed, liked to change gold ingots these days, thought Remo as he searched for a working pay phone.

Still whistling, Remo walked to the next terminal. He would call Chiun when he found a pay phone that worked. Chiun would lend him some money. Normally he would have asked Smitty, but Smith would probably ask for collateral and Remo was wearing all the collateral he had to his name.

There was no answer from Chiun's room, so Remo asked the operator to switch him to Dr. Smith's office.

"Remo," Smith said. "I'm glad you called."

"You are?" said Remo. "Think about that a minute. I still don't work for you."

"I need you here, right away."

"Nothing doing," said Remo. "I'm retired. No more missions, no more killing."

"Are you familiar with the landing of the *Yuri Gagarin?*"

"No, but I can hum 'Sink the Bismarck.' "

"Don't be smart, Remo. Chiun was just brought into Folcroft. There's something terribly wrong with him, and I have reason to believe it is related to the missing Soviet space shuttle."

"Chiun?" whispered Remo, gripping the receiver until he left fingerprints embedded in the plastic.

"Folcroft doctors are examining him now."

"He might be faking," Remo said slowly. "He did that once before. At least, I think he was faking that last time."

"I don't know, Remo. It looks serious. And Anna swears it's connected with the *Gagarin* mystery."

"Anna? Is that your wife's pet name this week?"

"No. Anna Chutesov. You remember her."

"Oh, her. Was she asking for me?"

"As a matter of fact, yes."

"Did you tell her I was engaged?" Remo asked in an anxious voice.

"No, I didn't think it was important."

"Try to break it to her before I get there, Smitty. I don't need any more problems right now."

"Please hurry."

"Don't hang up yet, Smitty. I'm out of money. Can you arrange airfare for me?"

"Go to the Winglight Airlines desk. A ticket will be waiting for you there. Where are you, by the way?"

"Seattle."

"First class or coach?"

"First class," said Remo. "You must really need me, Smitty. In the old days, I never had a choice."

"I expect you to reimburse me for the fare, of course," said Dr. Harold W. Smith.

"Of course," parroted Remo Williams. "National security is only national security, but the Folcroft budget is forever." And he tossed the receiver to the floor and walked away.

11

Remo Williams brushed past the secretary.

"I'm sorry, sir. Dr. Smith is in conference," the secretary said.

"He'll see me," Remo snapped, tight-lipped.

The bosomy woman jumped to her feet and put her head into Smith's office one step ahead of Remo Williams.

"I'm sorry, Dr. Smith, I couldn't stop him," she apologized, getting out of Remo's way just in time.

Dr. Harold W. Smith saw the rock-hard face of Remo Williams and said, "Quite all right, Mrs. Mikulka. No one could."

"Where is he, Smitty?" said Remo. "Where's Chiun?"

Anna Chutesov rose from her corner seat.

"Hello, darling," she said in a warm voice. She walked up to give him a welcoming hug and found herself clutching empty air.

"Hi," Remo said without glancing in her direction. To Smith he repeated his demand. "Chiun. Take me to him."

"This way, Remo," said Smith. He led Remo to the elevator.

Anna Chutesov stood rigid, disbelief marking her unblemished complexion. When she realized she was being left behind, she ran after the pair and squeezed through the closing elevator doors. Remo was in a heated conversation with Smith.

"He's regained consciousness and is asking for you,"

Smith said. "The doctors are certain he will be all right."

"Then what was the problem?" Remo wanted to know.

"Better let Chiun explain it to you."

Remo stared at the ceiling light, flexing his thick wrists impatiently. "He'd better not be faking this time. He just better not be," Remo warned. But the sick worry on his face belied his harsh tone.

"He is not," said Anna crisply.

"How would you know?" asked Remo distantly, as if months had not passed since they had said warm farewells to one another.

"I was with him when it happened."

The elevator doors slid open, and without waiting, Remo brushed past Anna Chutesov as if he had suddenly forgotten they were talking.

He found Chiun sitting up in a hospital bed. The visage of the Master of Sinanju was waxy and pale, but Remo's attuned hearing told him Chiun's heartbeat and lung action were normal.

"Little Father, what happened to you?" Remo asked.

"Death," said Chiun hollowly.

"You're not dead," said Remo.

"I am not dead," agreed Chiun. "Not yet. But I do not matter. Sinanju is dead. The future is dead. It is gone, all of it gone."

Remo, hearing the trembling anguish in the voice of the Master of Sinanju, knew that his mentor was not faking. The pain was real. Remo sat at the edge of the bed, took Chiun's long-nailed hand in his, and pressed it concernedly.

"Tell me all about it, Little Father," he said.

"There are many deaths, Remo. There are the death of body and the death of mind and the death of spirit."

Remo nodded. Smith and Anna Chutesov hovered in the open doorway, reluctant to intrude.

Chiun turned his hazel eyes upon Remo's deep brown ones.

"But there is a worse death than any of those," he intoned. "Woe to the House of Sinanju. I shall rue the day I allowed that woman to lure me into that place of doom."

"Woman?" wondered Remo, looking at Anna Chutesov. He looked right through her as if she weren't there. Anna flinched under the indifference of his gaze.

"I was learning to drive a motor carriage," Chiun explained. "Do not trouble yourself that you were too easily bored to complete your teaching. I understand. You were too busy seeking the unfindable homeless to care for your adopted father, who spent nearly two decades training you in the sun source. A few hours of instruction in return were too valuable to you. But it is of no moment. I understand."

Remo squeezed Chiun's hand.

"Cut it out, Chiun. I don't want to hear guilt. I want to hear what happened."

"The Russian woman lured me into the diabolical temple with the Russian name. She promised the Master of Sinanju a few moments of diversion from his cares and worries. But before it was over, I felt it die within me. All of it."

"Die? What died?"

"The future of Sinanju."

"I am the future of Sinanju. Haven't you always said that?"

"You are the future of my house, Remo. But not of the pure line. The pure line ends with me."

"That's news?"

"Tell them to be gone," Chiun said, gesturing in the direction of the open door.

Remo turned. "Could you two give us a minute? This is family stuff." And Chiun smiled wanly.

"We'll be in my office," said Smith. Anna went reluctantly, her features a patchwork of confusion. Remo was ignoring her.

When they had gone, Chiun laid his aged head against the double pillows.

"Lean closer, my son, that I may speak of my misfortune. It is too unbearable to say aloud. I will whisper it."

Puzzled, Remo leaned his ear next to Chiun's thin mouth.

"I can no longer have children," the Master of Sinanju intoned in a doleful hush.

Remo looked blank. "Children?"

Chiun nodded. "The seed within me has died. It is the fault of the Russian woman—her and that place of death."

"Seed?"

"Yes, seed. You know, Remo. The male seed. The seed that makes the female fat with child."

"Are you trying to tell me you're impotent?"

"Shhh! Do you want the whole of Folcroft to know of my shame?" Remo saw the color come back into Chiun's cheeks, but it was buried beneath the skin, like roses under wax.

"Little Father," Remo said gently, "these things happen. You get older, you slow down, things change. I don't think it is so terrible."

"So terrible!" Chiun hissed. "Is there wax in your white ears? There can be no offspring of my bloodline. It is over. When I awoke from my fevered sleep, I knew it instantly. The seed no longer burned within my loins. Alas, no woman will ever bear it now."

Remo stood up."

"Little Father, I think I understand your disappointment. But as long as I've known you, you've never expressed any interest in having children. I always thought I was sort of . . . well, you know."

A gentle light sprang into the eyes of the Master of Sinanju. "You are, Remo. But you are not the blood of my blood. Oh, there is some Korean in you. We both know this. But you are not the product of the pure seed of Sinanju."

Remo shoved his hands into his pockets. "I'm sorry if that disappoints you, Chiun. But I thought I was good enough."

The Master of Sinanju reached out to touch Remo's arm. "Do not be hurt, Remo. There is being a son and being a son. I think no less of you than I would if my dead wife had birthed you in the shadow of the Horns of Welcome itself."

"Then what's the problem?"

"The problem is that my seed has died."

"So, it died. You weren't planning on remarrying, were you?"

"Phaggh!" Chiun spat. "No. One disappointment of a barren wife was enough. But the seed of Sinanju was there, should I have had need of it."

"For what? A sperm bank?"

"You're being insulting, Remo."

"Okay, okay. I just don't understand the fuss. You seem to be fine. I'm thrilled. That's all I care about."

"Typical," clucked Chiun. "You think only of the moment, not of the future. Very well, I will explain it so that even your dense brain will absorb the true import of this calamity."

Remo folded his arms. "I'm listening."

"I am the last of the pure line of Sinanju. You are the next Master, not of the pure line, but you will do."

"Thanks," Remo said dryly.

"I mean no insult. You have done well. For a white. But Sinanju is not merely the skills, not only the sun source. It is a blood tradition that has been passed down the line of my ancestors for centuries."

"It fell apart when you could find no relative worthy of training," Remo said. "That's how I came into the picture."

"An oversimplification—but what can I expect from one of your mentality? Try to follow along now. You are the next Master of Sinanju. When I am dust, you will take my place. But suppose something were to happen to you?"

"You'd have to start all over and train another, I guess."

"I am too old for another uphill struggle with a grown pupil. If you were to perish, I would have to start with a babe, which is the traditional way to train a future Master. Preferably a Korean. More preferably of my village, and even more preferably of my seed."

"I get it," said Remo suddenly. "If I were out of the picture, you'd try for another son."

"Yes," said Chiun. "Exactly." Then his voice trailed off. He looked at Remo suspiciously.

"What do you mean—*another* son?" Chiun asked.

Flustered, Remo tried to cover up. "I meant another son, like me. I'm your son, sort of."

"That is not what you meant, Remo. Speak to me."

"I know about the son who died," Remo admitted.

"How?" said Chiun, sitting up. "I have never told you that story."

"True," Remo admitted.

"Have you been looking through my personal scrolls?"

"Never," said Remo, crossing two fingers over his heart and giving the Boy Scout salute.

"What, then?"

"The Great Wang told me. It was one of the things we talked about when his spirit appeared before me and I passed into full Masterhood."

"That gossip!" hissed Chiun. "He was always a gossip."

"Hey, that's no way to speak of the dead. Not to mention the greatest Master in the history of Sinanju."

"I do not wish to discuss it."

"I understand, Little Father. Maybe someday you will. Maybe someday you will see me as the son fate denied you."

"I would rather see you as the avenger of the seed of Sinanju."

"You want revenge, huh?"

"It is your duty. Our duty."

"I'm game."

"We must be careful," said Chiun, raising an admonishing finger. "I do not want you to lose your seed too."

"Oh, don't worry about me," Remo said airily. "I think I have a few good years left in me."

"You have not listened to a word I have said. This is not a calamity of aging, for I am still young in Sinanju years, but of deliberate evil. Someone did this to me. He is doing it to others. We must stop him."

"Okay," Remo said, still not following Chiun. "We'll stop him."

The Master of Sinanju sank back into the bed and closed his eyes wearily. "He has ears, but he does not understand," he muttered.

Anna Chutesov was hitting a high C when Remo walked into Smith's office.

"I am telling you that someone has perpetrated a heinous crime against my country," she railed.

"Calm down, Ms. Chutesov. I understand your frustration, but your theory is not . . . plausible."

"I know what I know."

"And I know nothing," Remo interjected. "Somebody fill me in."

Anna Chutesov presented Remo with her shapely back. Remo ignored the slight.

"Ms. Chutesov thinks she has found the Soviets' missing space shuttle."

"Thinks!" Anna blazed. "I know."

"Stenciled letters on an inside wall are not exactly conclusive proof," said Smith dryly. He was seated behind his big oak desk. The computer terminal was up from its concealed port and running. Smith had sent his secretary off on an errand. He was uncomfortable conducting CURE meetings in his office, but he had no choice.

"It was the *Gagarin*," Anna Chutesov insisted. "Why else would it have the same name?"

"What's the *Gagarin*?" Remo asked.

"Ms. Chutesov is here on authority of her government to recover their missing shuttle, which may have crashed in this area."

"I got that much," Remo said.

"The shuttle is named *Yuri Gagarin*. She thinks she's found it."

"I *have* found it," Anna Chutesov bristled. "It is now called the Yuri Gagarin Free Car Wash."

Remo looked at Smith and silently made circles over his temple with a finger. He mouthed one word behind Anna's cool back: crazy?

Smith shook his head in the negative.

"That doesn't sound right," Remo said.

Anna whirled on him. "What would you know, you . . . you *sukin syn*?"

"Hey," Remo said in a hurt voice. "What happened to détente? And the good times we once had?"

Anna sputtered something unintelligible.

"Did you tell her?" Remo asked Smith.

"No time," Smith said. "It never came up."

"What never came up?" Anna demanded.

"My new situation," Remo said, suddenly understanding Anna's bad mood. She had expected to pick up their casual relationship where it had left off months ago. She didn't know about Mah-Li. "Never mind," Remo sighed. "I'll fill you in later." To Smith he said, "I think Chiun will recover. He claims that he's been sterilized."

At Remo's words, Anna Chutesov sank into a chair and buried her face in her hands. "He knows," she said. Her shoulders shook uncontrollably.

"I thought you said you didn't break the news to her," Remo said doubtfully, looking at her.

"I did not," Smith affirmed.

"Then what?"

"Ms. Chutesov is convinced that the shuttle has been reconstituted as this Yuri Gagarin Free Car Wash. She and Chiun drove through it. That was when Chiun lapsed into unconsciousness. Her story is patently absurd, of course. The shuttle crashed two days ago. Assuming some idiot was inclined to build a car wash out of the scrap, he could hardly have accomplished that feat overnight. But there is something odd about the car wash."

"That's the temple of evil Chiun was babbling about? A freaking car wash?"

"It seems so," said Smith.

Remo went over to Anna Chutesov and gently shook her shoulder.

"Is that it?"

Anna Chutesov lifted a tear-filled face to Remo's. She shook her head until her blond hair flopped at the nape of her neck.

"He must have killed the crew," she said brokenly. "There is no other explanation."

"Could I see you a moment, Remo?" Smith asked.

Remo and Smith huddled in a corner.

"I don't understand any of this," Smith said.

"Join the club."

"The *Gagarin* disappears near Rye and then this woman shows up. She's the only one outside of our operation who knows about CURE."

"You think this is a setup?"

"Her car-wash story is ridiculous. And why was Chiun rendered unconscious and she was not?"

"Sinanju makes a person more sensitive to certain things that don't bother normal people," Remo said. "The hamburger you had for lunch would put me six feet under. I do know this much: if Chiun says he was sterilized by a car wash, I have to believe him, Smitty."

"I think you should look into that car wash, Remo. Take Ms. Chutesov with you, but keep an eye on her."

"Gotcha," Remo said, making an A-okay sign with his fingers.

Remo rejoined Anna Chutesov, who had found her feet and her composure. She wiped her eyes with her fingertips.

"You game for another crack at that car wash?" Remo asked.

Anna Chutesov squared her shoulders and opened her mouth to speak.

"Yes," said the Master of Sinanju from the doorway. He was wearing a hospital johnny, which he clutched at the back, out of modesty.

Remo snapped around.

"Little Father, should you be out of bed?"

"It is my future that has been murdered, not my resolve," said Chiun. "And I cannot allow you to venture into that evil building without me to guide you. For you lack the wisdom of the full Master and are the last potent vessel of Sinanju, Remo."

"I never thought of myself in those terms." Remo smiled.

"Neither have I," said Anna Chutesov archly.

12

Remo slowed the car as they approached the crude road sign that said YURI GAGARIN FREE CAR WASH.

"Where are the huge lines I've been hearing about?" he asked. He had driven the car from Folcroft because Chiun was too weak to fight about it. Anna Chutesov smoldered in the back seat. At times, she dabbed at her eyes. Remo, feeling a wave of pity, thought he knew why. Anna was hurt by his rejection of her. Maybe she was in love with him. He would have to break the news of his engagement to her gently, poor kid. Let her down easy.

"There!" Chiun said, pointing. He had donned a tiny suit of green and white checks that made him look like the Korean version of a racetrack bookie. "The place of evil," Chiun added. "Fie on the day I set eyes upon its wickedness."

"Looks like an ordinary car wash to me," Remo ventured.

In the back seat Anna Chutesov growled from the back of her throat and unlimbered a Walther PPK automatic from a pocket of her spring coat.

"Where'd you get that?" Remo asked, noticing the gun in the rearview mirror.

"I bought it."

"How'd you manage that? Guns are tough to get in this state."

"The gun-store owner was very co-operative. He, at least, recognized me for what I am."

"A Russian agent?" Remo asked.

"No, fool. A woman."

"Oh," said Remo. "I think there's something I should tell you."

"Later," Chiun broke in. "The evil place looms ahead."

Remo coasted to the bottom of the ramp, letting two cars pass before he slid onto the grounds of the car wash. There was no activity about the place. The wind shook the banks of oak trees behind it. There was a cardboard CLOSED sign taped to the front.

"Looks deserted," Remo said after a long pause.

"A brilliant observation," Anna Chutesov snorted, stepping out of the car, pistol in hand.

"Hey!" Remo said. "Wait up!"

"Hush!" said Chiun. "Let her do as she will."

"She might get killed," Remo pointed out.

"Better her than us. Besides, it is her fault I have been unmanned."

"Unmanned? Oh, right."

"Let us see how the car-wash machine treats her," Chiun said.

"Nothing doing, Little Father," Remo said. "She might do something crazy." Remo trotted after her.

Anna Chutesov had stepped into the open entrance. She moved like a cat, supple and silent, and Remo felt, vaguely, a stirring of his old feelings for her. She was a graceful female animal, cool as a snow leopard, and fearless. She paused before the hanging leather strips to examine a control board.

The leather strips lifted quietly like the tendrils of a great plant and wrapped around her head, arms, and legs. Anna Chutesov screamed as they dragged her inside.

Remo broke into a run.

The Master of Sinanju pounced after him and got in his way.

"No, Remo!" said Chiun, pushing against Remo's stomach. "I will attend to this. You must not risk your seed too."

"You're not well. You stay."

"We will both go, then, stubborn one," Chiun said, and they flashed into the Yuri Gagarin Free Car Wash. They went through the hanging leather strips so fast they cracked like sails in the wind.

Inside, Remo saw an incredible sight. The interior of the car wash was dark, hot, and stifling, but its mechanisms were alive. Looking down the length of the car track, he saw frantic mechanical movement. It was like a fun-house tunnel come to malevolent life.

Huge bundles of hanging strips of leather, like seaweed, dragged along the wet flooring, and out of the tangle poked a pair of slim legs. Anna's legs. And Anna screamed as they dragged her toward the flailing machinery.

"Hold!" Chiun cried. Remo, his eyes automatically adjusting to the light, saw the Master of Sinanju jump to one side of the leather tangle. There was a flurry of flashing fingernails, and in a twinkling, the leather strips fell into a wet heap.

Remo helped Anna Chutesov to her feet.

"Good going, Little Father," said Remo. "I have her."

"Now take her," Chiun cried. "I demand you leave. Go! This instant!"

"Nothing doing," said Remo stubbornly.

"The danger is not at this end," Anna said suddenly, "but at the other."

Remo and Chiun looked at her. She was dripping wet.

"How do you know that?"

"Trust me. I know," said Anna, wringing out her hair.

"What do you think, Little Father?"

Remo never heard what Chiun thought, because suddenly jets of water sprayed at them from all directions and the huge spinning buffers bore down on them.

"You take the right side, Remo. And I will take the left," said Chiun.

"And you follow us," Remo told Anna.

Remo moved to one side as the buffer, red and blue like a child's ball, came at him suspended on the end of a strut mechanism.

Remo went for the strut, avoiding the buffer, which, despite its size, looked harmless. But Remo knew those bristles, designed to scour enameled car bodies, would tear off his skin in a twinkling.

They never even got close.

Remo hit the strut at the lug point and sent the buffer flying into a wall. It bounced off, teetered like a rolling tire, and wobbled to the ground.

Remo looked back. The Master of Sinanju was still occupied with the twin of Remo's buffer.

Chiun had set himself off to one side, his feet apart in a fighting stance, as the whirling pom-pom of plastic came at him.

"Stand back," he said.

"What is he doing?" demanded Anna, her voice on edge. "He is just standing there. He will be killed."

But the Master of Sinanju was not just standing there. His hazel eyes were fixed on the whirling device. When it was a whisker's length from his face, he stepped back and pushed out both hands, the fingers held loosely, as if he were a magician throwing flash powder onto a brazier.

The heavy bristles encountered Chiun's long, Sinanju-trained fingernails.

It was no contest.

The buffer spun like a buzz saw, but it was a buzz saw that had lost its teeth. Red and blue bristles flew off in all directions like rice at a wedding. Wet, they coated the walls and floor.

Anna screamed.

Chiun laughed at the sight of the Russian woman pawing at her clothes. Snippets of bristle clung to her, making her look like a human ice-cream cone sprinkled with red and blue jimmies.

"I warned you to stand back," Chiun said.

Remo took Anna by one arm and spun her in place, and although his hands moved as if he were slapping her body at high speed, Anna felt nothing more than the fanning breeze of his hands in motion.

When Remo stepped back, there wasn't a speck of plastic on her clothes.

"Thank you," she said formally.

"Stick close," Remo advised.

"The soap is next," Chiun pointed out. "It will come from those nozzles ahead."

Remo nodded. "Let's hit them before they hit us."

"Agreed," said Chiun. Still sticking to opposite sides of the track, Remo and Chiun went for the vertical bars which housed the jet nozzles. No sooner had they begun to dribble than fingers clamped over them with the power of hydraulic vises. The nozzles, crimped by the steel-strong fingers, dripped white liquid that burned holes in the concrete flooring.

"They use strong soap here," Remo said.

"Fool," said Anna Chutesov. "Do you not recognize acid when you see it?"

"What's next?" asked Remo.

"Don't you know?" asked Chiun. "I thought all whites were familiar with machines."

"Not all car-wash machines are alike. And I've never been in this one before."

"The hot-air things," said Chiun.

And then they came, dropping from the ceiling to the height of a car hood, and blowing hot air.

"We can walk around those," Remo said casually. "They won't hurt us."

"You are too confident," warned Chiun.

"Car washes are built to clean, not to kill," Remo said.

The blowers suddenly gushed flame.

"This one does not appear to know that," reminded Chiun, sidestepping a jet of liquid fire.

Remo grabbed Anna.

"What are you doing?" she yelled.

"Trust me," Remo said, pulling her into the mounting flames. They went through the sudden wall of flame. The Master of Sinanju, executing a nimble leap, joined them.

"I could have burned to death," Anna said angrily, shaking free of Remo.

"No chance," Remo said, looking back at the abating flames. "You're covered with water. It protected you."

Suddenly the air was alive with death.

"Down! Hit the floor!" Remo called to Anna. He recognized the sound of automatic-weapons fire. A bullet zinged past his face.

Remo heard the stutter of a machine gun to his right, outside the car-wash track. He tore through the latticework, avoiding the bullet spray easily.

The weapon was an M16 rifle attached to a mounting on the floor. It fired automatically. Remo came up on the side and snapped out the banana clip. The weapon ran empty. Silence returned to the dark confines of the building.

"Chiun, you and Anna stand still. They've got booby traps on this side. I'm going to check them out."

"Have a care, Remo," Chiun warned.

Remo found a complicated spring contraption designed to launch a trio of stun grenades when a photoelectric beam was intercepted. Remo extracted the grenades, crushed them into harmless powder in his hands, and wiped his hands clean.

There were no other traps ahead, so he clambered back onto the track.

"What did you discover?" Anna asked, her automatic shaking in her hand.

"Later. I want to check the other side. Give me a hand, Little Father."

Chiun reached into a tangle of pipe and gear mechanism and, at Remo's signal, they lifted a section of the wall free.

Remo stuck his head around the other side. It was dark, darker than the car track, but Remo's eyes took in even the tiniest light and magnified it until he could see clearly.

"This side looks clean," Remo said, rejoining the others.

"Did you see the letters?"

"Yeah. The letters C.P. Someone painted them on the wall at a funny angle. So what?"

"Look above you," Anna suggested.

Remo and Chiun looked up. Through a maze of piping they saw a huge red letter C. Another C. was beside it.

"Together they read CCCP," Anna said grimly. "In the alphabet of Russia, it stands for the Union of Soviet Socialist Republics. Exactly the same as the letters on the *Gagarin's* wing."

"Are you going to start that again?" Remo said. "This

is a car wash. It's been here for years. Smith told us that. It isn't your missing shuttle."

"It's just like a stubborn male to refuse the evidence when it is pushed in your face," Anna cried. "You are invincibly dense, like all your sex. How can I make you believe!" She looked overwrought, tense. Something was bothering her, Remo realized. Something more than the present situation.

"Try leveling with us," Remo said, on a hunch.

Anna bit her lip. She turned to the Master of Sinanju, who was watching the flames die out at the other end of the track.

"Do you remember the silver ball that hung over the exit from this place?" she asked.

Chiun wrinkled his face in thought.

"Ah, I remember now," he said. "I was looking at it when I lost consciousness. I remember wondering what it was for."

"It matches photographs my government showed me of a communications satellite that was aboard the *Yuri Gagarin* when it was launched."

Remo looked at Anna Chutesov as if she had two heads.

"Communications satellite?" Remo said. "Hanging in a car wash."

"Yes!" Anna said hotly.

"A communication satellite hanging in a car wash," Remo repeated, giving Anna a skeptical look.

"Why is that so unbelievable, Remo?" Chiun said. "Some people hang furry dice in their motor carriages. Perhaps it is an American custom with which you are not familiar."

Remo looked at Chiun. And again at Anna.

Finally he shook his head. "All right, all right, we'll go look at this thing. But let's skip the rest of the tour, shall we?"

"It is unbelievable," Anna whispered, touching the huge red letters as they brushed past them.

"It's nothing," Remo said. "In the sixties, kids would spray graffiti letters twice that size. Right-side-up, upside-down, and inside-out. They called it pop art, but I think they were all on drugs or something."

"American teenagers would write USA, would they not?"

"Probably members of the Socialist Workers' Party," Remo said. "This is about their speed."

They emerged at the end of the building. A door led off to one side, back in the direction of the car track.

"Probably leads to the exit," Remo said.

"The man in the booth may be there," said Anna. "And the satellite. I am sure he is making the machinery attack us."

Remo turned to Chiun. "What do you think, Little Father?"

Chiun listened. "I hear no heartbeats. Just water dripping."

"Then let's go," Remo said, reaching for the doorknob.

"No!" said Anna Chutesov. "Let me go first."

"Why?"

"It is too late for me. But you have not been affected. I will go first."

"Affected?" Remo said.

"The woman speaks wisdom," said Chiun. "She will go first."

Remo shrugged. "Then she goes first. But let's pick up the pace. I haven't got all day."

Anna unlatched the safety to her automatic, gripped the door with her other hand, and set herself. The door flew open and she was through it in a smooth leap. Her heels clicked on the opposite side.

"See anything?" Remo asked.

"No," Anna said in a small voice. "It is gone. Gone."

Remo went to step over the threshold, but Chiun tugged him back by the sleeve.

"I am next. I will tell you if it is safe."

The Master of Sinanju sniffed the air carefully before venturing forth. Remo waited. He knew that sniffing the air was the last resort of a Master of Sinanju when facing the unknown. It was a legacy from the days when Masters traveled through faraway lands, often encountering unknown carnivores along the way.

Chiun went through. In a moment he called for Remo to follow.

Remo found Chiun and Anna staring at the ceiling. Strutwork dangled brokenly. It was clear that something, not long ago, had hung from the ceiling, but had been twisted loose.

"There was something there, all right," Remo admitted.

"See?" Anna said triumphantly. "I told you. And there, that is the booth where the man with the sinister voice called to me."

"What did he say to you?" Remo asked.

"He said, 'Have a nice day.' "

"Gosh, that's sinister, all right," Remo said. "I'll ask Smitty to put out an all-points bulletin. Charge him with inciting to have a pleasant day. He could get twenty years for that."

"It was the way he said it," Anna insisted.

Remo stepped over to the grimy booth and rubbed his fingers against the glass. Some gunk came off in his hands, but the other side was just as dirty and he couldn't see clearly.

"Funny," he said. "This place is as new as a penny, all except for the dirt on this thing."

"The owner's booth," Anna told him. "He did not wish to be seen, the fiend."

"The demon car washer," Remo said. "I don't buy it."

"How do you explain the machines that attacked us?"

"Malfunction," said Remo.

"And the booby traps?"

"The owner has a thing against trespassers," said Remo, less confidently.

"Fool," said Anna Chutesov. But even her scorn did not faze Remo Williams.

Remo pulled back his hand and hit the glass with an open palm. The glass shivered, hung in place as spiderweb cracks radiated from the point of impact, and then fell in shards so fine it was as if the glass had turned to sugar.

There was a control board on the other side, Remo saw, and the entire booth appeared to be occupied by it. There was no space in which a human being could sit. Indeed, no seat. Just a steel well lined with cables and connective devices.

"You say there was somebody in this booth?" Remo asked.

"I saw his shadowed outline through the glass," Anna insisted.

"Have a look," Remo offered.

Anna stepped carefully. When she saw that the confines of the booth could contain a human being only if he had no lower body, she turned a pale greenish white and stumbled off to a corner, where she sank to the ground, unmindful of the grease stains her clothing soaked up.

Remo yanked handfuls of thick cable until they snapped apart. The sound of the frantic machinery ceased immediately. He turned to Chiun.

"Did you see the outline too, Little Father?"

"Would you think me mad if I said yes?" asked Chiun.

"No."

"I did."

"That's crazy!" Remo blurted.

"Liar!" Chiun said.

"Okay, I'm sorry. It just doesn't add up."

"It's diabolical," said Anna. "Where can it be? What can he be doing with it?"

"I think Anna's starting to lose it, Little Father. Listen to her."

"You listen to her. I am disappointed that I have found no one on whom to avenge my honor." And he kicked at a wall until the bricks tore loose from their mortar. After Chiun had a pile, he stamped the bricks with his sandaled feet until a fine powder resulted.

"Feel better now?" asked Remo.

"No," replied the Master of Sinanju.

"I didn't think so," said Remo, offering Anna Chutesov a hand. "Let's all get out of here. There's nothing more to this shell."

They walked out the back and around to the car.

Before they got to it, the windshield fell out in pieces and the hood popped up.

"Uh-oh," said Remo. "We're in trouble."

"Sniper," cried Anna, diving for shelter behind the car.

"That too," said Remo, looking around. "But I was thinking of what Smitty is going to say. That's his car."

A tire exploded, and one side of the car sprouted a string of neat black holes like notes on a musical scale.

On the ground, Anna clung to handfuls of grass and wondered what was keeping Remo and Chiun from joining her in safety.

In the budding top of an oak tree, Earl Armalide emptied an M16 rifle into the car until he knew it was undrivable.

He dropped the weapon, which swung free from a lanyard attached to his belt, and unshipped his AutoMag

pistol from its shoulder holster. He decided to take out
the tall skinny one first. His head represented the
cleanest shot.

Armalide fired one round. He was so sure of his aim
that he didn't pause to look. He assumed his target had
gone down, and adjusted his sights to the second target, the little Oriental in the Pee Wee Herman suit. A
second shot blasted out.

Earl looked for the girl next. She must have sought
shelter behind the car. No problem. An AutoMag round
could go through an engine block. He brought the
pistol back up to his face, but in doing so noticed that
there were no bodies on the ground.

Now, where had those two kills gone? They couldn't
have dragged themselves behind anything. A .44 slug
had the stopping power to nail a kill to the ground,
even if death wasn't instant—which it usually was. Yet
there were no blood tracks or drag marks in the grass.

Earl Armalide had chosen this particular oak tree
because it was solid and had a large crown of branches.
There wasn't much leafage to the branches this early in
the spring, but there were enough green buds to help
his camouflaged body blend in. It was also high enough
that he could pick off anyone attempting to climb the
tree after him.

The tree, all four feet in circumference of it, shook
suddenly.

Earl Armalide was sure it was an earthquake until he
looked down.

Looking back up at him from the base of the tree
were the upturned faces of his two kills. But they
weren't dead. They were alive. In fact, the tall one with
the dead-looking eyes smiled. It was not a nice smile.

"Ollie, ollie oxen free," the tall one called playfully.

"Eat this, sucker," Earl spat back. And then he fired
into that grinning face.

The bullet split a half-buried rock where the man had been standing. The tree shook again. More violently this time. Earl had to clutch at the tree trunk just to hold on. Sap made his fingers sticky and he cursed. That stuff could jam a fine weapon like the AutoMag in no time. He switched hands.

"Why do you not come down?" asked a high squeaky voice.

Earl looked down at the Oriental and shot at his face.

The oak shook again. Although the Oriental had not seemed to move, he was suddenly standing in a different spot. Unharmed.

"He must want us to say the magic word before he'll come down," the tall man told the Oriental in a loud voice.

"I wonder what it is?" said the Oriental in a wondering tone.

"Maybe it's 'timber.' " The tall man called up to him, "Hey, buddy, is it 'timber'?"

Earl did not answer. Instead he pulled the pin from a hand grenade and dropped it.

The hand grenade shot back up. It stopped an inch from the tip of Earl Armalide's quivering nose. It seemed to hang in the air as if weightless. Frantically Earl made a grab for it, but the grenade suddenly fell back.

It returned in another millisecond, hanging impossibly.

"I can keep doing this until it goes off in your face," the tall man sang cheerily.

Earl grabbed again. In vain. The grenade fell. The next time it came up, Earl was certain the five-second fuse had been exhausted. But the grenade did not stop long enough to eradicate his sweating face. It kept going.

High up, it went off. The concussion shook the tree. Hot pieces of shrapnel rained down. They clipped branches, set bark to smoldering, but miraculously, did not embed themselves in Earl's huddling flesh. A single red-hot piece landed in his lap and he frantically pushed it off before it burned through to the family jewels.

"Are you coming down now?" the Oriental wanted to know. He slapped at the trunk and it vibrated like a sapling.

Earl clung to the tree, hoping it was all a dream. It had to be. No one could toss a grenade into the air so high that the shrapnel lost its killing velocity falling back to earth.

"I guess it's 'timber,' " said the skinny white man.

And the mighty oak shook again, and kept on shaking.

They were using axes on the tree, Earl knew. The sharp, meaty *thunk* sound was unmistakable. So was the *crack!* just before the oak began to sway.

Earl jumped clear as the oak crashed to earth. He landed in a tangle of breaking branches, and lay still, the air knocked out of him.

The white man and the Oriental extracted him from the woodsy mess. Earl Armalide sat catching his breath as the two stood over him.

Dazed, unable to think of anything better to say, he asked, "Where are your axes?"

"What axes?" asked the white man, blowing a wood shaving out from under a fingernail.

13

The first thing Dr. Harold W. Smith said when he arrived at the Yuri Gagarin Free Car Wash was, "What happened to my car?"

"He shot it up," Remo said laconically, indicating a man in soiled jungle fatigues.

Smith stood over Earl Armalide, who was crouching on the grass, his hands clamped at the nape of his neck.

"I'm not giving you anything but my name, rank, and serial number," said Earl Armalide. His arms ached. His legs tingled from constricted blood flow. He would have moved to relieve the agony, but after the white guy had forced him to assume the humiliating POW position, the Oriental had touched him at the back of the neck, and ever since then Earl Armalide had felt as if he had developed a case of muscle lockjaw.

"Your wallet," Smith said grimly.

"I already checked," Remo said, handing Smith the billfold. "There's no I.D."

Smith took the wallet wordlessly. He riffled through it, found no identification cards, and extracted a thick sheaf of bills. He silently counted out an assortment of tens and twenties. He tossed the wallet at the man's feet and said, "This is for the damage to my car. And estimated towing charges."

"I hate to point this out, Smitty," Remo said, "but you've got a more serious problem on your hands than your repair bill. Besides, anyone can see your car has been totaled."

"I know an excellent mechanic," said Smith. "Now, what was so urgent that you insisted I come here personally?"

"This guy is somehow connected with the car wash. He says his name is Tex Trailer."

"He's lying," said Smith. "His name is Earl Armalide."

"How do you know?" Remo demanded.

"I recognize him from TV reports. He's a federal fugitive, wanted on a number of charges, not excluding murder of law-enforcement officers." Smith leaned down and broke the man's dog tags from under his camouflage collar. He glanced at them briefly.

"See?" he said, showing them to Remo.

Remo read the tags. "You're right. It says Earl Armalide, serial number 334-55. What branch are you with, buddy?" Remo wanted to know.

"No comment."

"Turn it over, Remo," said Smith.

Remo read the other side. Stamped on the reverse were the words "Compliments of *Survivalist's Monthly*."

"They give them out as a subscription promotion," Smith said. He walked over to the car-wash entrance and examined the exterior carefully. With a penknife taken from his vest pocket, he pried loose one of the white tiles covering the outer walls.

"Interesting architecture?" asked Remo when Smith returned.

"No, but the construction materials are unusual."

"You should see the washing mechanism itself. It'll kill you."

"It's unusual to see space-age plastics and top-secret alloys used in the construction of a commercial car wash," said Smith levelly, looking Earl Armalide straight in the eye.

Earl Armalide wanted to look down to avoid Smith's stern gaze, but his neck would not move.

"What are you saying, Smitty?" Remo asked.

"This is no ordinary tile. It is one of the expensive heatproof tiles used to protect shuttle hulls. They are easily identified. They resist extraordinarily high temperatures, but are so brittle that they would shatter under heavy rain." To demonstrate his point, Smith broke the thick tile between two fingers. "I believe Ms. Chutesov was right all along," he added, dropping the pieces at Armalide's feet.

"I am glad someone here can think," said Anna Chutesov. She, too, was giving Earl Armalide a hard stare.

"Where are the crewmen?" asked Smith.

"Search me. I never saw them. I think they're dead."

"Of course they are dead," said Anna dully. "They were brave men. They would never let one man take control of their craft without fighting to the death."

"I had nothing to do with that," said Armalide. "The ship was empty when I climbed aboard."

"At Kennedy?"

"Yeah. I figured it was a Russky invasion trick and if I stormed the shuttle I'd be a hero and get a pardon from the President."

"Idiot male," spat Anna Chutesov.

"If the ship was empty, pal, who flew it?" Remo demanded. "You don't look like you could fly a paper airplane if you had the rest of your life to practice."

"This is gonna be hard for you folks to swallow."

"Try us," Remo said.

"There wasn't anyone inside."

"It took off automatically?" asked Smith.

"No, not exactly."

"What, exactly?" Remo prompted.

"The ship flew itself," Earl Armalide said.

The Master of Sinanju drifted up behind the crouched figure of Earl Armalide. "Did I mention that this was the creature who worked at the evil car wash? No? As such, he is partly responsible for the unspeakable thing that has befallen the House of Sinanju. As reigning Master, I claim the right to deal with the wretch as I see fit after this interrogation is over."

"And I claim the right to kill him in the name of the brave Soviet cosmonauts who lost their lives," returned Anna Chutesov.

"The ship flew itself!" said Earl Armalide frantically. "You gotta believe me."

The Master of Sinanju reached for Earl Armalide's left ear and gently rubbed it between thumb and index finger. He continued rubbing it even after Earl Armalide gritted his teeth against the rising heat friction. Smoke drifted past his nostrils. He was sure the old Oriental was cooking his earlobe with a match, but there was no flame visible. And Earl Armalide had spent years training his peripheral vision in simulated combat. He could tell if his sideburns lined up without using a mirror. But he could not see any match.

"What say you now?" said Chiun.

"The ship flew itself," Earl Armalide moaned through watering eyes. "It was alive."

"Okay, the ship flew itself," said Remo, who knew that no one ever lied under the fierce pain the Master of Sinanju could inflict. "Tell us more."

"I climb into the ship, you understand? Only there's no one aboard. I'm in this airlock thing and suddenly the walls start closing in. You know, like in an old movie when the hero is locked in a secret room by the bad guy."

"Impossible," scoffed Anna Chutesov. "The airlock has no such function."

"Don't I wish," said Earl Armalide. "I was this close to becoming a bouillon cube, when—"

"Did you say cube?" asked Smith, suddenly thinking of the objects found on the Kennedy Airport runway.

"Yeah, cube. The walls were coming in and so was the roof. I figured if they didn't stop, I'd be cubed. But they did stop. In fact, the ship asked me a question. I look up and there's an eyeball sticking out of a wall. It's looking at me, and it wants to know about this magazine that fell out of my pocket—*Survivalist's Monthly*."

"What did the . . . er . . . ship want to know?" Smith asked.

"It wanted to know what a survivalist was. It was interested in survival."

The hair on the Master of Sinanju's face suddenly trembled, but there was no breeze to stir it.

"What did it ask?" Chiun wanted to know.

"About survival stuff mostly. It wanted to compare notes. It said it was a machine, a survival machine."

Smith, his face ashen, looked at Remo. "Are you thinking what I'm thinking?" he said hollowly.

"Gordons," said Remo. "He's back."

"Who's Gordons?" asked Anna Chutesov.

Chiun nodded grimly. "Gordons. Oh, this is a doubly evil day."

"Who's Gordons?" repeated Anna.

"You saw him?" Smith asked Earl Armalide. "Can you describe him?"

"I told you. I just saw the eye. He claimed that he was the shuttle. Said he assumilated it."

"Assimilated," corrected Smith. His face was haggard.

"Yeah, that."

"Did he give you his name?" Smith asked.

"I didn't know he had one. He said he was a survival machine and if I helped him, he wouldn't cube me. It was a good deal, so I took it. I wasn't interested in being on a first-name basis."

"Explain the car wash," said Smith. "It's the *Gagarin*, isn't it?"

"Must be. One minute I was inside the ship, flying along calm as you please. The next, we landed and I was knocked cold. When I woke up, I was inside the car wash and the ship was gone. I figured I was home free at first, but when I tried to leave, the place came alive. You can't imagine what it's like, being threatened by a car wash."

"Oh, I don't know," Remo said dryly.

"That's right," Earl Armalide said sheepishly. "You do."

"Why a car wash?" Smith asked.

"Camouflage. At first, I gave him the idea that if he didn't want anyone chasing him, he had to be unobtrusive."

"The Yuri Gagarin Free Car Wash is not exactly a masterpiece of subtlety," said Remo.

"That part came later. He kept the name because, to be truthful, he didn't seem too bright. Know what I mean? He took things too literal. I tried explaining that the name was a problem, but he said he had to work with the things he assimilated. First he assimilated the shuttle, then he merged that with the car wash. When the military dropped their search, he was ready to move on to something else, when the idea hit him."

"What idea?"

"Well, he was afraid of enemies. I guess that's you guys, because he talked about you a lot."

"Oh, Gordons and I go back years," said Remo.

"Who is Gordons?" Anna asked again. She was ignored.

"He said as long as there were so many people on this planet, he wasn't safe. I kinda understood him then for the first time. I'm a survivalist, you know. We had that in common. The way we figured it, there were too many people on the planet telling others what to do and using up all our resources. There were people after me and other people after him. So we decided to team up to solve the problem."

"By sterilizing the planet," said Anna Chutesov.

Remo, Chiun, and Dr. Smith all looked at Anna Chutesov in the same blank way.

"Yeah? How'd you know that?" Armalide said wonderingly.

"Yes, how did you know that, Ms. Chutesov?" Smith asked firmly.

"Let him tell it," said Anna Chutesov. She looked pale. Her Walther hung slack in her hand as if it was suddenly too heavy.

"There was this satellite thing that came with the shuttle, the Sword of Damocles," Earl Armalide said. "The machine had figured out it used microwaves to sterilize people—only he didn't call people, people. He called them meat machines. Isn't that weird? He and I figured out that if we kept killing our enemies, it only made more enemies. But if we sterilized them, all we had to do was wait them out, and in time, we would have the problem licked."

"The Yuri Gagarin Free Car Wash was a sterilizing factory?" Smith said, aghast.

"The free part was my idea," Earl Armalide said proudly. "You get more people faster that way."

"Did it never occur to you that a single car wash, at best, is only going to get a fraction of the population in, say, a fifty-mile radius?"

"After a while, yeah, it did. I explained that to the machine, and we worked it out. Once we figured out how to make more microwave sterilizers, he was going to give me the franchise. I was going to have free car washes all over the world."

"Wonderful," said Anna Chutesov, throwing up her hands. "Capitalism at work."

"Don't knock it if you ain't tried it, honey," Earl Armalide said.

"Who was in the booth?" asked Remo.

"The machine, I guess. He could turn into anything. I guess he turned a part of the car wash into a mechanical man. I never saw him clearly, though. He never came out of that booth. But I was glad about that. I got tired of air ducts talking to me and eyeballs staring from walls. It was creepy."

"So where is Gordons now?" asked Remo.

"He got spooked. He said he picked this area because he knew his enemies—that's you guys—were near here, and he figured if he waited around long enough you'd drive through, and zap—he'd sterilize you both. Only the Oriental came through alone and he panicked when you were knocked out, mister."

"I am not a mister, I am a Master," said Chiun, his face full of repressed rage. He slapped Earl Armalide's head and the man, paralyzed in a fetal position, tipped over like a tenpin.

Remo set him up again.

"Sorry, Master," Armalide said. "When it happened, he figured it was time to split because he was worried you'd probably investigate what happened to your friend. He didn't want a fight. So he had me steal a garbage truck for him so he could get away. I was to wait until you people showed up. You know what happened after that."

"He's driving a garbage truck?" Smith asked.

"No, he *is* the garbage truck. It was the only thing I could hijack that was big enough to carry the satellite so no one'd notice it."

"Where did he go?"

"He didn't say. But I figure he's out there doing his

thing, sterilizing people. He wants to clear the planet of meat machines. You know, people."

"That's insane," said Anna.

"No, ma'am, it's survivalism in its purest form. You get rid of the people and you got no problem. No more wars, no more racism or nuclear fears, and plenty of food to go around. It was going to be just him and me."

"It would take, minimum, about eighty years for the last living adult to die off," Smith pointed out.

"We had it figured at fifty," said Earl Armalide. "In fifty years, the only ones on their feet would be so old we could shoot most of them. Can you guys make my arms and legs work again? I'm ready to go to jail now."

"No chance," said Remo.

"Okay, I'll go to jail like this."

"That wasn't what I meant," Remo said meaningfully. Chiun looked at Smith. "Emperor?"

"We're done with him," Smith said. "Make it look like an accident."

"Would you prefer heart attack or perhaps sudden lung collapse?" asked Chiun, fluttering his fingernails over Earl Armalide's close-cropped head.

"Hey, you can't do this. It's against the Geneva Convention. Besides, I ain't killed no one. I just sterilized a few. Show me a law against that. Specifically."

"You are forgetting the IRS agents and the others," Smith reminded him.

"Hell, that was different. That was war."

Those were the last words that Earl Armalide ever spoke because Anna Chutesov, her face like something extracted from a granite cliff, stepped up to the squatting survivalist and shot him in the face.

Earl Armalide rocked back on his heels and tipped over onto his back.

"What did you do that for?" asked Remo. "Now we're

going to have to bury him so there won't be an investigation."

"You do not understand, do you?" Anna Chutesov said furiously. "Idiot! You are so immersed in your own stupid self that you overlook the obvious."

"Give me a hint."

"I, too, have been sterilized."

"Is that why you've been so upset?" Remo asked.

"Of course. What did you think?"

"Never mind," said Remo, who was suddenly disappointed to learn that Anna Chutesov wasn't carrying a torch for him, after all.

14

"Who is this criminal, Gordons?" demanded Anna Chutesov.

They had returned to Smith's Folcroft office. Outside the big picture window with a view of Long Island Sound, night had fallen. There was no moon. The only illumination came from the weak fluorescent lights, fluttering out their last hours. The office looked danker than it did by day, and Anna Chutesov notice the dust in the corners that was not apparent in sunlight. Of course, she thought to herself, Smith probably cleans it himself. It was, after all, a high-security office. And Smith had a mania for attending to details himself.

Upon entering the room, Smith immediately took his customary position behind the desk and brought up the CURE terminal. It glided up from the solid oak desktop like a genie answering a summons. Smith went to work.

Anna turned to Remo and Chiun.

"Will one of you kindly answer my question?" she asked.

"Anna wants to know about Gordons, Little Father," Remo said.

"Pah! Do not speak that thing's name to me," Chiun spat.

"Anna's not a thing," Remo said. "And I don't think you should blame her for what happened to you. She got a burst of microwaves too."

"I did not mean the female," said Chiun. "I was referring to the machine man."

"Oh, Gordons. Right."

"Will someone answer me?" Anna said tartly.

"Gordons is an android," Remo said. "Do you know what an android is?"

"Yes," answered Anna Chutesov.

"Good," said Remo. "Why don't you explain it to me? I never got it straight." He took a lotus position on a bare space on the floor. Chiun had settled onto a hardwood chair. Anna thought to herself that they had their positions reversed. It should have been Remo on the chair and Chiun on the floor.

"An android is an artificial human being," said Dr. Smith absently, keying commands into his terminal. "It's a quantum leap above a robot. An android can be made to look like a human being with artificial skin and prosthetic devices."

"Thank you," said Anna Chutesov. She regarded Remo as if he were a bug.

Remo, stung by the look, sat up straighter.

"We first encountered Gordons years ago," he said seriously. "His full name is Mr. Gordons. He was named after a brand of gin. Gordons was part of some crazy space program—an artificial thinking machine designed to pilot spacecraft on long-range missions, where it was impossible to send a man. He was programmed to survive, no matter what. I guess that program was a good one because he's still around. We thought we killed him at least three times."

"I wish we had," snapped Chiun.

"Go on," said Anna Chutesov.

"Anyway," Remo continued, "Gordons was just an experiment. Before him there was Mr. Smirnoff, Mr. Seagrams, and others. The NASA scientist who created him liked to drink. A lot. That was the inspiration for naming him. Then the government cut off funding for the project and Gordons overheard. He understood that money was important, and must have figured he'd be deactivated or something, so he fabricated a new look to pass himself off as a person and escaped."

"How could a machine replicate a person?" Anna asked.

"He usually tears the skin off and starts from there."

Anna, in spite of herself, shivered.

"A monster," she said. "When will you males stop creating such monsters? When?"

"Actually," Remo said, "the NASA scientist was a woman. What was her name, Chiun? Wasn't it Vanessa Something?"

"Yes, you are correct," Chiun said disinterestedly. "Vanessa Something was her name."

From his console station, Dr. Smith broke in. "A records search indicates that the city currently owns the car wash. It went bankrupt in 1984 and was seized by the state for taxes."

"How did this Gordons take control of the *Gagarin*, in the first place?" Anna asked.

"Smitty, what can I tell her about that?" Remo asked.

"Whatever you want. After what we've heard about the microwave satellite, she's hardly in a position to complain."

"Complain about what?"

"Gordons had everything he needed to survive," Remo went on. "He was as strong as a derrick and could transform himself into anything. He might even be that chair you're sitting on."

Anna Chutesov jumped up and looked at the chair. It looked ordinary, a simple wooden chair. Then it moved.

Anna recoiled.

"It's him! Gordons," she screeched.

"Look at her, Remo," said the Master of Sinanju.

"She is afraid of a chair." And he stamped his sandaled
foot against the floor a second time, causing the wood
chair to skitter to one side. Chiun cackled.

Anna Chutesov gave the Master of Sinanju a bilious
stare. But when she sat down, she availed herself of
another chair.

"Gordons was missing one critical element," Remo
went on. "Creativity. He didn't have any. He could
reason in a simple way, but he was unable to think
original thoughts—kind of like a Hollywood producer.
It drove him crazy. He kept trying to figure out ways to
become creative. One time, he killed a bunch of artists
and scooped out their brains for study. It didn't work.
The last time we saw Gordons, he had assimilated a
NASA artificial intelligence computer. And, bingo, instant creativity."

"But he was still stupid," said Chiun.

"Slow, anyway," Remo amended. "But he was still
dangerous, and we had to chase him all the way to
Moscow to recover the computer."

"Gordons was in Russia?" Anna Chutesov said.

"Do you remember the *Volga* missile?" Remo asked
her.

Anna Chutesov said nothing. She realized her mouth
was gaping, and she clicked her teeth shut.

"That is one of the greatest secrets of my government. How did you know about it? How could you
know?"

"Your people had a doozy of an idea. They couldn't
land a man on the moon, even after the U.S. showed
them how. And they were afraid that we'd claim the
moon for America one day. So they created a deadly
germ that could breed in space and infiltrate spaceships
and spacesuits, and then loaded it aboard a moon rocket
called the *Volga*. The idea was to poison the moon so
no one could claim it."

"I know the plan, said Anna Chutesov hotly. "It was insane. But it was a previous regime. The current leadership had nothing to do with it."

Remo shrugged as if that were a minor detail. "Chiun and I followed Gordons to Moscow. The Russians had captured him because in order to launch the *Volga*, they needed the artificial intelligence computer he had absorbed. We made a truce with Gordons, and convinced him to ride the *Volga* into outer space and send it off course. The moon was saved and Gordons was out of our lives. A happy ending, we thought. Until today."

"There were strange rumors surrounding the *Volga*'s fate," Anna Chutesov said slowly. "The men in charge of the project were blamed for the failure and executed."

"That's the biz, sweetheart," Remo said.

"I do not understand how this Gordons could attach himself to the *Yuri Gagarin*. The *Volga* was lost in deep space."

"That part I can't explain," admitted Remo.

Smith suddenly looked up from his terminal.

"Oh, my God," he whispered.

"Smitty?" said Remo.

"Gordons knew where to find us."

"Yeah, he's creative now. He probably looked us up in the Yellow Pages."

"No. That isn't it." Smith turned in his chair to face the others. "Even lost in space, Gordons wasn't entirely helpless. He probably fabricated some kind of propulsion system from the *Volga*'s parts. It would be easy for him. But finding earth would be next to impossible without specific navigational programming. Unless Gordons had a signal to home in on."

"What's so hard about that? There's plenty of earth radio transmissions he could have locked in on," said Remo.

"Not from Rye, New York. Not from Folcroft."

"From where, then?" asked Remo.

"Do you remember the transmitter Gordons planted on you that last time?"

The memory made Remo absently scratch his back.

"Yeah, he stuck a little thing into my back no bigger than a bee sting. I didn't even feel it, but it threw my body out of whack. I couldn't stop hopping like a jack-in-the-box until Chiun pulled it out."

"You never could sit still," Chiun said unkindly.

"I took possession of the device after you returned from Moscow," Smith said. "It later disappeared. I can remember thinking it must have fallen off my desk and I had accidentally swept it up during a cleaning."

Anna Chutesov came to her feet.

"If this Gordons homed in on this office, it would explain why he landed in this area," she said.

"Yes, it would," Smith agreed.

"Then the transmitter must still be here. Where did you see it last?"

Smith considered. "Right . . . here," he said, placing a finger on a packet of printouts. "I placed it on a set of computer forms. I always put my printouts on this quadrant of the desk."

"Believe him," said Remo. "At home, he's probably got individual compartments in his sock drawer."

"Then the transmitter is still here," said Anna.

Everyone got down on the floor and looked for the transmitter, except the Master of Sinanju, who muttered something about closing the barn door after the horse. Only he didn't say "horse," he said "ox."

After several minutes, Remo got to his feet and said, "I don't see anything."

"Nor I," admitted Smith.

"It does not seem to be here," said Anna Chutesov. And remembering that Remo had called it a bee sting, she ran her hands along the floorboards. She was rewarded by a tiny stinging sensation in the ball of her thumb.

"Ouch!" she said deliberately.

"You all right?" asked Remo solicitously.

"A splinter," Anna said, getting to her feet.

"Here, let me . . ."

"I am fully capable of extracting a splinter from my own hand," she said sternly. Turning to Smith, she asked, "Is there a washroom where I can clean the wound?"

Smith handed her a brass key. "Use my private washroom," he said. "It's out in the hall."

"Thank you," said Anna Chutesov.

In the washroom, she held her thumb up to the bare ceiling bulb. As she had hoped, the splinter was black, insectlike. It had penetrated at a shallow angle so that it was clearly visible under the translucency of her epidermis. The transmitter.

Anna washed a droplet of blood from the point of entry and, without removing the transmitter, she rejoined the others.

"Find it?" she asked brightly.

"No," said Smith.

"Uh-uh," seconded Remo. "I don't think it's here."

"I'll have the room swept electronically," Smith decided. "A bug is a bug. I'm certain it will be found. I should have thought of it before this."

"Don't be too hard on yourself, Smitty," Remo said. "Who would have thought Gordons would return?"

But Smith wasn't listening. He was at his terminal again, tapping keys like some demented concert pianist.

"What're you doing, Smitty?" Remo asked curiously.

"I'm setting up a program to collect statistics on infertile couples. It will feed off the AMA computers and Health and Welfare files."

"You're going to track Gordons that way?"

"No, this is in case you and Chiun don't stop him before he succeeds in sterilizing more people. I can count on your help, can't I?" said Smith, thinking of Anna Chutesov's promise to influence Remo into solving the *Gagarin* mystery.

"Sure," said Remo. "I promised Chiun I'd pitch in on this one. And I have six months to kill before returning to Korea."

"This could take much longer to resolve than six months," Smith warned.

"How long?"

"Weeks, months, years," said Smith. "We don't know what form Gordons will take next. But based on the car-wash experience, he will probably assume the form of a commercial structure, something through which large numbers of people pass daily."

"Like an airliner?"

Smith shook his head. "Not efficient enough. Something stationary. A skyscraper, or possibly the Lincoln Tunnel. The World Trade Towers, perhaps."

"You're talking about a needle in a haystack here," Remo protested. "Chiun and I can't just walk up to every big building on the continent, tip our hats, and ask, 'Pardon us, but are you Mr. Gordons, the sterilizing machine?' "

"When we find the transmitter, we should be able to track him through it," Smith said. "It's our only lead."

"Okay," Remo said, settling back onto the floor. "So we wait."

"Wait!" cried Anna Chutesov. "Thousands of people are being sterilized with each passing hour and you want to wait! Does he not understand what is happening?" she asked no one in particular.

"No, he does not," said the Master of Sinanju. "He cannot understand. He thinks it is some unfortunate minor ailment, like a hangnail."

"What'd I say?" said Remo plaintively.

"For every person who loses the ability to procreate," Smith said, "the world not only loses the 2.3 children most couples bear in their lifetimes, but also the grandchildren and great-grandchildren and so on who will never be. Future leaders, scientists, entertainers, and ordinary hardworking people will never be. The loss to our social and economic future is incalculable. If Gordons only partially succeeds, Americans may become scarce in the next century."

"Smith is right," said Anna Chutesov.

"I'm glad you said that, Ms. Chutesov," said Harold W. Smith, "because I would like some information from you. Please give me the specifications on the microwave satellite. I believe that Gordons' survivalist accomplice referred to it as the Sword of Damocles."

"I regret I cannot," said Anna Chutesov. "That is a state secret."

Smith nodded imperceptibly and returned to his computer.

"Do any of you know the Russian words for 'Sword of Damocles'?"

"*Damoklov Mech*," answered the Master of Sinanju.

"Thank you," said Smith, keying the phrase into his computer. He waited, and in a matter of seconds he was reading an on-screen file.

"The Sword of Damocles is a phased-array microwave transmitter," he reported. "It's very powerful, capable of affecting a massive landmass during an approximately four-year orbital sweep. As you may know, microwave ovens heat by exciting water molecules in food. This satellite uses the same principle to raise the human body temperature just enough to neutralize the reproductive system. Slow but certain sterilization results. The transmitter is very powerful, but for it to accomplish its full task, the sterilizing of America, it must be

placed in orbit. That part at least is good news. On the
ground, Gordons can do limited damage. But we're still
talking thousands of people each month, under opti-
mum circumstances. And Gordons, being a machine,
has no limitations on his lifespan. If not stopped, he
could conceivably sterilize the entire earth."

"Where are you getting that information?" demanded
Anna Chutesov, blinking furiously.

"From the computer files of the Glavnoe Razvedyvatelnoe
Uprevlenie," Smith said nonchalantly.

"You . . . you have access to GRU files!"

"Normally, no," Smith admitted. "I am usually re-
buffed by the obstructive passcodes placed over the
files. But knowing the codename Sword of Damocles
makes it possible to penetrate this particular file."

"When did you obtain this capability?"

"Recently. I've been working on it in my spare time.
Oh, don't worry. I'm sure you'll inform your superiors,
and they'll enter new buffers. Just be certain you don't
tell them about my operation."

"And if I do?"

"You know I could not allow you to live under those
conditions," said Smith without hesitation.

"I will not allow this woman to be killed until she has
fulfilled an obligation which she has incurred with the
House of Sinanju," said Chiun sternly. "Afterward is a
different matter."

"What obligation is that?" asked Remo.

"It does not involve you," said Chiun, eyeing Anna
Chutesov and shifting his gaze to Remo suggestively.

Anna came over to Chiun's side and whispered in his
ear. "What would you have me do?"

"Remo liked you before," Chiun breathed back. "Get
him to like you again. Offer him anything, but extract
from him a promise to remain in service to America."

"I will do my best," said Anna. She drifted over to

Remo, who had been watching the exchange with open-faced curiosity.

"Hi!" said Anna Chutesov breathily. She smiled.

Remo smiled back tentatively.

Anna placed her slim hands on his bare biceps and almost purred. "I was thinking that when this is over we should get reacquainted."

At the familiar stroking, Remo felt a delicious tingling deep within him. Memories of Anna Chutesov, the soft Anna Chutesov, the one who was a tiger in bed, rushed back to him.

Suddenly Anna Chutesov felt her hands clutching themselves instead of Remo's hard arms.

"Bad idea," Remo said sheepishly.

Anna allowed herself a moment of puzzlement, then pressed closer.

"Perhaps we could discuss this outside," she breathed.

"I can't," Remo pleaded.

"Yes, you can. Help him overcome his shyness," said the Master of Sinanju. "He has grown very shy lately."

"Little Father, did you put her up to this?" Remo asked.

"Never," said Chiun.

"How could you say such a thing, my Remo?" asked Anna Chutesov. She had met Remo's earlier indifference with scorn. That had not worked. She had ignored him and he had ignored her back. She had insulted him, to no avail. Now she was throwing herself at him. That never failed.

Until now.

"Look, things are different with me now," Remo said.

"I will make them right again," said Anna, playfully tugging on Remo's belt. She laughed. Her pink tongue darted out from between perfect teeth and her blue eyes sparkled mischievously.

At his desk, Smith's face flushed and he craned his head closer to the computer screen.

Remo backed away, his hands held palms-up before him, as if Anna Chutesov were some species of poisonous fruit.

"I'm engaged," Remo blurted out. "To be married."

"So?" asked Anna Chutesov.

"I love her."

"You will have all the rest of your life to love her. Love me now."

"Could you please take this out in the corridor?" asked Smith exasperatedly. Open displays of affection embarrassed him. Naked lust such as Anna Chutesov was portraying upset him even more.

"Yes, it is disgraceful," said the Master of Sinanju, who hoped that in the privacy of another room, it would be even more disgraceful.

"I don't want any part of this," said Remo. "I'm going to be a happily married man soon."

"I do not believe you," protested Anna Chutesov.

"Look, don't take it personally," said Remo. "There's just someone else now."

Anna Chutesov looked at Remo, his hard-muscled arms, his lean stomach, and that face that could be so cruel but now had that little-lost-boy look, and experienced a sinking feeling deep within her. Remo no longer wanted her.

Suddenly, clearly, Anna Chutesov realized something that had been true for a long time, but which she had pushed deep into her subconscious.

She wanted Remo Williams. She wanted him sexually, wanted him so badly it made her throat dry and her heart pulse hotly in her neck, and if he were not stronger than she was, she would have flung herself at him, tearing at his clothes until she got what she wanted.

Worse, she thought she loved Remo Williams.

Remo Williams, who did not want her.

In one moment of shocked recognition, the entire psychological mindset that had enabled Anna Chutesov to rise to political power crumbled like a sand castle before the inrushing tide.

Anna looked at Remo with uncomprehending eyes.

"I want you, but . . . but you do not want me," she said hollowly.

"I'm sorry. Really," Remo said, meaning it.

Biting her lower lip like an injured child, Anna Chutesov walked stiffly out of the room.

"You both saw that," Remo said. "I tried to break it to her gently, didn't I? It's not my fault she couldn't handle it."

"You gave her the back of your hand," said Chiun angrily. "And after all she has meant to you."

"She'll be back," said Smith hopefully.

"No, she will not," said the Master of Sinanju, folding his hands into the oversize sleeves of his jacket. "She wanted only two things, Remo and Gordons. Remo has spurned her. She will go directly to Gordons and take her bitterness out on him."

"How can she?" asked Remo. "She doesn't know where to find Gordons any more than we do."

The Master of Sinanju shook his aged head. "Not so. She has the insect thing."

"Gordons' bug? How?" demanded Smith.

"She picked it up, pretending it was a splinter. Did neither of you notice? She was so obvious about it."

"You could have mentioned it, Little Father. Now we have to follow her."

"We do not need the insect device. I know where Gordons is."

"You do?" Remo and Smith said a beat apart.

"Yes. Gordons wishes to make all persons barren. He

will thus go to the only place where he can accomplish this easily.

"Where?" asked Smith.

"The one place in all the world where all Americans and non-Americans go. Or hope to go."

"Where?" asked Remo.

"I will not tell you. I will show you. Emperor Smith, I will ask you to make travel arrangements for Remo and myself."

"I would like to know exactly where you are going," said Smith.

"The matter between Gordons and the House of Sinanju is a matter of honor," Chiun said gravely. "Remo and I will handle it."

"Very well," agreed Smith. "I will make the arrangements. Just let me know the necessary details."

Just then, the red telephone rang. Smith picked it up.

"Yes, Mr. President. You picked an appropriate time to call. I have just confirmed the fate of the Russian shuttlecraft."

Smith listened.

"No, it is not intact, exactly," he said uncomfortably. "Actually, the crew is already in Air Force hands. No, the Air Force hasn't quite realized this as yet. I know it sounds strange, sir. In fact, the whole matter is strange. Please bear with me while I try to explain. And by the way, Mr. President, are you sitting down?"

15

Carl Lusk loved sex. He loved it in all its splendifer-
ous variety. In an age of AIDS, herpes simplex, herpes
complex, and more traditional social diseases, he moved
unafraid through the dating bars and computer love
services. Carl Lusk was twenty-three and believed that
AIDS only happened to fags and heroin addicts and that
only stupid people caught social diseases. While he was
young he was going to sleep with as many women as
possible. Sometimes as many as five in one day. The
trick, he believed, was not to sleep with the same
woman twice. He knew the chance of catching any
social disease from a one-night stand was slim, but it
went up with each subsequent encounter. As Carl saw
it, monogamy was like playing Russian roulette with
five of the six chambers loaded.

Carl Lusk was not completely reckless. There were
some encounters he did avoid. Dogs, children, and
men were at the top of that list. But that didn't mean
that he couldn't fantasize about these things. To that
end, he put together one of the world's largest collec-
tions of taped and print pornography to facilitate his
fantasizing.

Carl was a baggage handler at Denver's Stapleton
Airport. It was not the most glamorous job in the world,
but it enabled him to copy off women's names and
addresses from the luggage he loaded. It was better
than a computer dating service. Cheaper, too. Carl

Lusk was ferrying a load of luggage to a waiting 747 when the garbage truck that would change his entire attitude toward sex rolled past him.

Carl knew right away there was something strange going on.

First, garbage was not picked up on the runways, where the jets sat.

Second, there was no one driving the garbage truck. The driver's seat was empty.

Carl spun the baggage truck around and lost the rear cart of the baggage train, but he didn't care. He was sure the garbage truck was out of control and he wanted to see where it ended up. Carl also liked to stop at major traffic accidents.

The garbage truck went around a corner to the area where private planes were hangared, and Carl had visions of Piper Comanches flying in all directions.

When Carl negotiated the same corner, he was surprised to see that the garbage truck had come to a full stop.

Carl came to a full stop too.

The garbage truck had stopped behind a Lear jet, its front bumper touching the tail assembly.

Then the garbage truck reared up on its back wheels. The wheels spun and the garbage truck lurched like a rogue elephant. It came down on the Lear jet, squashing the tail and pushing its nose into the air. The garbage truck began to shake furiously. The Lear quivered like a fish caught in a net.

Carl Lusk watched in rapt awe. Under his breath, he said the first thing that came to mind. "Oh, my God, they're screwing!"

Carl Lusk got down on the runway and tried to look under the garbage truck's chassis. He had never seen a garbage truck screw a corporate jet before. He wondered what the garbage truck—which was obviously the male—had for equipment. Details like that fascinated him.

As he watched, gravel digging into his cheek, Carl heard the truck's hydraulic equipment start to grind.

"I wonder if that means it's coming?" he asked himself.

Then he saw it. A silver ball, like a perfectly round egg, dropped from the garbage truck's undercarriage and was absorbed by the jet. The jet's aluminum skin just opened up and swallowed the silver ball.

The garbage truck, suddenly quiescent, fell over on its side, rear wheels smoking and spinning impotently.

The Lear jet suddenly whined into life and rolled onto the runway.

As it passed, Carl Lusk saw that there was no one piloting the aircraft. Not only that, but the crumpled tail was returning to its normal shape like a plant recovering after being stepped on.

After the Lear jet had vaulted into the sky, Carl Lusk summoned up enough nerve to approach the garbage truck.

The driver's seat was vacant. But he knew that. The truck smelled of week-old trash and tiny bugs crawled out from the smeary edges of the hydraulic door, which hung open and empty.

"It's dead," Carl Lusk whispered. And then he thought about what he had just said. Funny that he would think of the garbage truck as dead. Garbage trucks did not live. Garbage trucks also did not copulate with other machines, but this one had.

Carl Lusk retreated to his baggage cart and decided not to mention what he had seen to anyone. On the way back to his terminal, he decided to burn his pornography collection. It would be tough to live without it, but maybe there was such a thing as too much sex after all. That left only the future course of his sex life to be decided—monogamy or celibacy? It was a grim choice. Perhaps he would flip a coin.

When the unauthorized Lear jet landed at Burbank Airport in California, it taxied to one end of the main runway and whined to a stop.

Because it had refused radio contact, did not ask for landing clearance, and came down the wrong way, the tower naturally assumed it had been hijacked.

Airport security was immediately mobilized. The first man on the scene was Officer Andy Ogden, who drove his car to the jet and got out cautiously. He did not draw his gun. He assumed that a drawn gun would be a signal for violence and he was trained to defuse violent situations, not make them worse.

As he approached the jet, Andy Ogden heard a loud metallic sound, like a titanic punchpress. There was no explosion, so he knew it was not a terrorist grenade going off.

A man came out from under the far wing. He jumped down as casually as if he had stepped from a barber's chair. The man walked up to Officer Andy Odgen.

He was not armed, so Andy Ogden did not pull his weapon. Pulling his weapon would have been an over-reaction. And Andy Odgen was trained not to overreact.

And so when the man with the strange silver suit and the fixed face approached him with an outstretched hand and said, "Hello is all right," Andy Ogden accepted the hand in relief as much as in friendship. When he saw that the man's face was a cluster of wires and circuits with glassy blue eyes and an armrest ashtray for a mouth, it was too late to draw his weapon because the man had squeezed his hand to a blood-soaked pulp and had started to work on his other hand.

His last thought was a strange one. Why did the man have a round porthole in the middle of his chest?

When the main security team reached the Lear jet, they did not think twice about having passed Andy Odgen on the way. Officer Ogden was driving his car, which for some reason had a great silver ball mounted on the roof. He was probably going for help. When they found the body on the runway, skinned raw, they forgot about Andy Odgen and drew their guns.

They recognized that there were times to overreact. They moved under the Lear jet's wings, looking for an open hatch.

They did not find an open hatch, exactly.

What they found was an opening in the far side of the hull. The opening was six feet tall, in the rough shape of a man, like the chalk outline usually made at murder scenes to indicate where the victim fell. It led directly into the ship.

They climbed in through the man-shaped opening and found that the plush passenger section was deserted. Going forward, they found that the cockpit had been vandalized. Most of the flight controls—the navigational instruments and on-board computers—were missing. They did not find the missing hull section, which should have been impossible to miss. Not only was it shaped like a gingerbread man, but there should have been a porthole in the middle of the thing.

The only other oddity was a television set built into one wall. It was on, showing a popular children's cartoon program. The chief of the security team turned it off and led his men back out to the body on the ground.

"Wonder who that thing was?" one of the others said.

The security chief looked at the inhuman carcass for a moment. He saw the gleam of white gold on the man's left ring finger and suddenly sat down on the runway.

"What?" he was asked when they saw his stricken expression.

"The ring. Look at the ring. That's Andy's ring!"

"You sure?"

"Look," the chief of security said in a sick voice.

One of the men looked. He saw the silver monogram A.O. mounted on an onyx setting. Bits of skin clung to the edges of the band, indicating that the epidermis had been torn off around the ring.

He too sat down on the runway. He threw up into his lap and didn't bother to clean himself off. He just sat there.

"That wasn't Andy we saw a minute ago," he said.

"I won't say anything if you don't," said the security chief.

The security team all sat down in a circle on the runway and made a pact that they would not mention the man they had seen fleeing the area who looked like their former colleague but was not. They cut their thumbs and pressed them together so that it was a blood oath.

Then they waited. But they didn't know what they were waiting for.

Anna Chutesov drove to the Soviet embassy in New York City. She drove over the speed limit because she felt that if she slowed down or stopped it would all catch up with her.

It caught up with her in New Rochelle. She pulled over to the side of the road and buried her face in the steering wheel and, for half an hour, sobbed uncontrollably.

When she sat up at last, her face was drawn and her eyes were dry. She was again the Anna Chutesov who had risen from the Komonsol to a position of supreme responsibility in the Kremlin.

She was in love. And the man whom she loved was not only an American agent but also, more damningly, he did not want her. It was the ultimate humiliation for a woman who had never before allowed herself the luxury of acknowledging deep feelings for any man.

The consul general was not surprised to see Anna Chutesov. He had been informed that she was in the country, and because he knew all about the missing *Yuri Gagarin*—as did the whole world by now—he assumed that the shuttle's recovery was her mission.

"Comrade Chutesov," he greeted unctuously.

Instead of speaking, Anna Chutesov took her thumb between her teeth and ripped at the skin. She dug at the tear with a colorless fingernail and attacked it again with her teeth.

"Here," she said, spitting a black plastic whisker into the doubtful consul general's hand. "This is a highly sophisticated homing transmitter. If there is a way to pinpoint the source that is receiving its transmissions, do so immediately and inform me once you have that information."

"Of course, Comrade Chutesov. Where might I reach you?"

"I will be in the embassy lounge. Drinking."

Anna Chutesov was drinking vodka when the consul general found her. She did not look drunk. Probably she wasn't. But the bottle on the bar was nearly empty.

"We have isolated the area at which the transmissions are directed," he said.

"Where?" snapped Anna Chutesov, pausing with a tumbler just under her elegant lips. The consul general noticed that there was no ice in the glass.

"In the state of California. Near Los Angeles."

"Is that the best Soviet science can do?"

"No. A team will be dispatched to triangulate the exact location, if that is what Comrade Chutesov desires."

"Comrade Chutesov only desires the loan of the equipment necessary to locate that point. Comrade Chutesov will handle the matter herself. Comrade Chutesov would not trust this to a man. Comrade Chutesov will never trust a man ever again."

"Yes, Comrade Chutesov," said the consul general. "You will not require backup agents on this matter?"

"I already have them, if the fools were able to pass themselves off as untrained migrant workers—which I think may have been too much for them."

And Anna Chutesov downed the remainder of the tumbler of warm alcohol, telling herself bitterly that all men were like straight vodka, colorless and so damned transparent.

16

Larry Lepper hated robots.

"I hate robots," he said.

"These aren't robots," said Bill Banana, head of the famous Banana-Berry Animation Studios, in a soothing voice. Normally Bill Banana saved his soothing voice for his girlfriends. When you were the head of the largest cartoon factory in the history of television, you did not soothe, you barked. Sometimes you did neither. Sometimes you just fired people when they refused to let you have your way.

Bill Banana did not want to fire Larry Lepper. He wanted to hire him. Larry Lepper, despite his youthful appearance, was the greatest animator in the business.

"I don't do robots," insisted Larry Lepper. "I did robots over at Epic Studios. You could fill a junkyard with the robots I designed for Epic. No more."

"These robots are different," soothed Bill Banana. He leaned back in his office chair, surrounded by life-size papier-mâché statues of his studio's cartoon creations. They looked more realistic than he did.

"I thought you said they weren't robots," said Larry Lepper.

Bill Banana spread his hands in an expansive gesture. He broke out in a pleased grin. Somehow, his grin looked wider than outspread arms. He had good reason to grin. When you grossed three million dollars a year and were responsible for exactly seventy-eight percent of the cartoons shown on Saturday morning, you were king of your industry. Even if it was an industry in which artistic skill, technical brilliance, and storytelling ability were reduced three percent each year as a hedge against rising production costs, so that after nearly thirty years of animation, the Banana-Berry Studio was reduced to cranking out cartoons that were only one step above flip-page books.

"They aren't robots. Exactly." Bill Banana grinned.

"Robots are robots," said Larry Lepper. "You can call them Gobots, Transformers, or Robokids, but they're still robots."

"*Robokids* made us a cool quarter-million last year," said Bill Banana seriously, rolling a stubby cigar to the other side of his mouth.

"The ratings sucked. You made it all on toy-licensing deals."

"That's where the action is these days. You know that. And don't knock *Robokids*. It was brilliant. I should know, I came up with it myself. Kids who transform into robots. No one had ever thought it up before. They had trucks that turned into robots and jet airplanes that turned into robots. They even had robots that turned into other robots. But *Robokids*? Original."

"I'm not working on robot shows," repeated Larry Lepper. "I'm sick of them. Here," he said, unzipping a black portfolio that was the size of an executive's desktop. "Let me show you my latest concept."

Bill Banana accepted the Bristol Board reluctantly. He looked at the drawing, cigar ash falling on the board with each puff.

"Buster Bear?" he barked.

"Look, this robot trend's gotta peak soon," Larry said eagerly. "Be the first guy out of the gate for a change."

"No good. No one will buy a Buster Bear toy. Look at him. He looks like a cream puff. Maybe we could change him, though. Call him Blaster Bear. Stick a whatchamcallit—an Izzy—in his paw."

"Uzi," said Larry Lepper wearily.

"We'll call it an Izzy. That way we can copyright the design and spin off the gun as a separate toy."

"And copyright the character yourself? Nothing doing," said Larry Lepper, snatching back the presentation piece before cigar ash burned holes in it. "Thanks, but no thanks."

"So let me tell you about my new show," said Bill Banana, happy to get Buster Bear off the negotiating table.

Larry Lepper wiped at his shiny forehead unhappily. He was only thirty-four, but he had already lost most of his hair. Oddly, his high forehead made him look younger than his years.

"No robots," said Larry Lepper.

"We call them Spideroids. They're not robots, exactly. They're giant spiders, see, but they turn into androids. An android is a robot that looks like a real person. My manicurist explained it to me."

"How original," said Larry Lepper dispiritedly.

"I knew you'd get it!" Bill Banana said excitedly, slapping the desk with a beefy smack. "I knew that you, Larry Lepper, of all the guys working in the industry today, would see the awesome potential of this concept. How fast can you come up with the designs? I'll put you on at our top salary."

Larry Lepper quietly zippered the presentation piece marked "Buster Bear" into his portfolio like a man closing the lid on his dreams.

"I'll do the model sheets," he said dully. "Get someone else to do the animation."

"Done," agreed Bill Banana, reaching across the desk to shake Larry Lepper's limp hand. He was not entirely happy, because it meant he'd have to hire other artists to do the stuff that Larry wouldn't, but it was dealable. He just wouldn't pay Lepper the top rate. The dumb schmuck hadn't worked for Banana-Berry in five years and would never know the difference.

"When do you need it?" asked Larry Lepper.

"Monday morning. The sponsors are gonna show up at nine."

"But this is Friday. I'll have to work all weekend."

"Work here. I'll give you a studio, have your food sent in, and if you want, a girl. Or a boy. Or both. I treat my employees right."

"Just leave me alone all weekend and I'll see what I can do," said Larry Lepper miserably, visions of drawing stupid robots for the rest of his life dancing in his mind's eye.

By Sunday evening Larry Lepper had generated a roomful of Spideroid model sheets, showing front and side views of different spider characters. He had jumping spiders, spinning spiders, and climbing spiders. There were brave spiders, mean spiders, and, for comic relief, silly spiders. They looked pretty sharp—if you liked spiders.

The problem was, Larry couldn't figure out plausible android transformations for any of them. Designing robots that became cars or planes was easy. But spiders had eight legs. Larry didn't know what to do with the extra legs. If he kept them, the androids still looked like spiders. And he couldn't ignore the extra legs. If the show sold, the model sheets would be turned over to a toy company for immediate production so that the toys would hit the stores the week the show premiered.

Larry tossed his pen into the inkwell in frustration. In his portfolio he had designs for dozens of funny animal characters which, if he had gotten them on the air twenty years ago, would have made him famous.

But Larry Lepper had not been an animator twenty years ago. He had been a child dreaming of drawing cartoons for a living and maybe, just maybe, owning his own theme park like his idol, Walt Disney. He never told anyone this, but Larry was more interested in operating his own version of Disneyland than he was cartooning. That was where the real money was. Animation was just the road to the greater dream.

Larry Lepper had pursued his dream—disappointing his father, who had had his heart set on Larry following him into the family hardware business—and come to Hollywood. He was good. But more important, he was fast. And he had found work.

Drawing robots that turned into motorcycles and flying saucers that became robots, all fighting mindlessly, and not a single human character in any of the scripts—that was the depressing part. If they wouldn't let him draw Buster Bear or Squirrel Girl or any of his other creations, at least they could give him a real-life person to draw once in a while.

Instead, he was stuck trying to come up with a plausible android counterpart for a giant spider with eight laser-beam eyes and vise grips for feet. He decided to work on the character's names instead. But even that defeated him.

"What the hell is another word for 'spider'?" he muttered aloud.

" 'Arachnid,' " said a metallic voice from the open door. "It is the scientific term."

Larry Lepper turned at the sound. There was a man framed in the door. He was a tall man, dressed in Hollywood pastels and wearing wraparound sunglasses that looked like they were part of his face and not an accessory. His shirt was open at the throat but instead of chest hair, Larry saw glass. Probably a medallion, but it looked pretty big. The man's hair was the color of sand, and when he smiled, it was like a camera shutter locking into the open position. His teeth looked too good to be true, even for Hollywood.

"Hello," said Larry Lepper, thinking the man was some assistant producer come to check on his progress.

"Hello is all right," said the man, walking in. He walked stiffly, as if his joints were arthritic.

"It works for me," said Larry dryly. Probably on coke, he thought to himself. Half the town was.

"I am looking for Commander Robot," said the man politely.

Larry extracted himself from his drawing board and distinctly heard two vertebrae pop. He had been hunched over the board since dawn.

"Um, he's not here," said Larry cautiously. And just in case this nut was dangerous, he reached for a sharp-nubbed Speedball pen.

"Lieutenant Cyborg, then," the man said calmly. The breeze wafting through the open window sent the man's scent toward Larry Lepper. Distinctive personal scents were in this year. On Rodeo Drive, where the stars shopped, you could buy colognes that made you smell like everything from avocados to old money. This guy smelled like the Las Vegas shuttle.

"Nope," said Larry. "I really think you should try the security guard at the front gate."

"He was most helpful. He directed me to this building. You are the only one here."

"He's not supposed to do that. We're normally closed on Sundays," said Larry Lepper, sliding toward the door.

"Yes, he was reluctant at first. I broke his arm in three places and his attitude changed. I have always been intrigued by the cooperative attitude caused by inflicting physical damage on meat machines."

"Meat machines?" asked Larry. The man was coming toward him, a hand outstretched.

"*Homo sapiens,*" said the man, taking Larry by one wrist. He exerted sudden pressure. With the Speedball, Larry stabbed him in the stomach three times. The Speedball broke on the third thrust. When Larry looked up at the man's face, that fixed smile had not changed one whit. It also seemed very far away.

Larry discovered that he was on his knees from the pain.

"What . . . what do you want?" he moaned.

"I have told you. I will ask again. I wish to speak with either Commander Robot or Lieutenant Cyborg. I have seen them on television fighting the Stone Kings and I wish to enlist their aid in combating two personal enemies of mine. I have lost my former tutor, who was a survivalist, and am in need of allies."

"You can't," Larry lepper groaned.

"Why not?"

"Because they're not real."

"I do not understand your meaning. I saw them myself on the television screen."

"They're cartoons. They don't exist in real life."

"According to your skin tension reading, you are telling the truth, but I still do not understand your words."

"I . . . I can show you," gasped Larry Lepper, feeling the two bones of his wrist clicking together in the strange man's one-handed grip.

Larry Lepper felt himself being yanked to his feet.

"Show me," the man said tonelessly.

"The next room," said Larry.

In the next room, Larry showed the man paintings of scenes from the *Robokids* show done on clear acetate. They festooned the walls.

"These are called cels," Larry said. "Artists paint pictures of Commander Robot and the others on them."

"This one is very realistic," said the man, plucking a cel from the wall.

"You gotta be kidding," said Larry Lepper, who had a low opinion of cel artists. He rubbed his sore wrist. The feeling was coming back.

"It looks exactly like Commander Robot."

"Well, yeah, that's true," Larry said. He picked a pile of cels off an acrylic-splattered worktable. "Here, see these others? The Commander Robot figure is different in each one. We shoot these in sequence so that Commander Robot seems to move against painted backgrounds. It's an optical illusion. It's called animation."

The man gathered up the cel paintings, and faster than it seemed possible, he sorted them into the correct order. Then, holding them up to the light, he fanned the cels until the illusion of movement was created.

"See?" Larry said hopefully.

"They do not talk." His voice sounded disappointed.

"They can't. They're just paintings. Actors dub in the voices."

"That would explain why Commander Robot and the announcer had identical voice recognition patterns."

"The actors double up. It's in their contracts. You must have a great ear to be able to tell that."

"Why is this done?"

Larry Lepper shrugged. "To make money, to provide entertainment for the children who watch the show. But mostly to sell toys and breakfast cereal."

"Is that your goal—to sell toys and breakfast cereal?"

"No, I just want to make enough money to launch my own business. I sank my savings into an abandoned theme park, but I need more cash to get it off the ground. That's the only reason I'm wasting my time on this junk."

"I am beginning to understand," said the man, letting the cels fall to the floor. "It is all make-believe. Yes, this explains another fact that had puzzled me."

"What's that?" asked Larry Lepper conversationally.

"Why Commander Robot and his fellow Robokids went to such great lengths to conceal their secret identities and then broadcast their adventures for all to see."

"I can see why that would bother you, pal. I sure am glad I was able to clear up the mystery for you. I sure am. Yes sirree."

The man stood in silence for a long time after he dropped the cels to the floor.

"You okay, pal?" asked Larry Lepper.

"Commander Robot and I would have made an effective team," said the man. His chin fell and even his too-square shoulders seemed to droop.

"You had a lot in common, yeah," said Larry. "Anyone can see that." The man was blocking the only path to the door and Larry knew he had to humor the guy. He might survive if he humored him.

"You understand," said the man, looking up.

"I'm good with robots," said Larry sympathetically. "Everyone knows that."

"Actually, I am an android survival machine. My name is Mr. Gordons."

"Glad to meet you, Mr. Gordons, I'm real sorry about the confusion. Real sorry. I'll ask the studio to put a disclaimer on the next episode so it won't happen again." Larry inched to the door. Mr. Gordons matched him step for step. Larry gave up.

"I appreciate your sympathy. Although I am a machine, I have the capability of feeling emotion. Also I can transform myself into any object with which I come in contact."

"Yeah, that's handy, all right. Real handy. Popular, too. I know lots of robots who can do that. Almost all of them, actually."

"I told you, I am not a robot. I am a survival android. My name is Mr. Gordons."

"Right. I got that. 'Robot' was just a figure of speech. No offense."

"None taken. Would you like to see me assimilate an object of your choice?"

"I really would, but I have to finish making Spideroids."

"What are Spideroids?"

"Cartoon characters. They're spiders who turn into androids."

"Would you like to see me become a spider, then?"

"No, not that," Larry said hastily. "I hate spiders. They crawl up my pants leg and make me itch."

"I would become a very big spider, and I would promise not to crawl up your leg if you do not wish it."

"Thanks just the same. Okay if I go back to work now?"

"I will watch you work," said Mr. Gordons. "Perhaps I will learn something useful."

"Suit yourself," said Larry Lepper, backing into the other room. He climbed behind his drawing board and pretended to get to work. Maybe the nut would get bored and leave.

Mr. Gordons watched him silently. He gave Larry the creeps, but he was afraid to make a break for it.

When Larry had not drawn a single line for five minutes, Mr. Gordons had a question.

"Why are you not working?" he asked.

"I can't think of a name for this one."

Mr. Gordons looked at the model sheet and the blank space at the bottom for the name.

"I am very creative. It is one of my newer skills. Let me try."

"Sure," said Larry Lepper, who couldn't get out of Mr. Gordons' way fast enough. "Go right ahead. I'll get lunch."

"Wait. I will not be long."

"Took me all weekend to do all those sheets," said Larry Lepper, and then he stopped talking.

The right-hand fingers of the man who called himself Mr. Gordons blurred suddenly. One minute he was touching the tumbler of ink pens on the desk, and then the next, he had an assortment of drawing utensils for fingers.

As Larry Lepper watched, slack-jawed, Mr. Gordons began writing names onto the model sheets with his index finger, which was a pencil. He inked them with his other fingers, which ended in different size nibs. His thumb was an ink eraser, but Gordons never resorted to it. He seemed incapable of drawing a false line.

Less than a minute after he began, Mr. Gordons handed a stupefied Larry Lepper a neat stack of model sheets. Larry went through them, his eyes bulging like those of a thyroid patient.

"Gobblelegs, Spinner, Spiderette," Larry read. "These are pretty good names—considering industry standards these days."

"Thank you. I also took the liberty of modifying some of your designs so that they are more practical."

"We usually don't worry about that stuff. The animators can't be bothered to keep the characters consistent half the time."

"Is there anything else?"

"Can you do the android robot counterparts? I'm having trouble with that part."

"You are my friend so I will do this for you," said Mr.

Gordons, and taking several blank sheets and ten minutes' time, he produced a set of model-sheet androids that exactly matched the Spideroid drawings.

Larry Lepper was astonished. This Gordons character didn't even refer to the original sheets. Yet his robots were perfect. They looked like they could be built. In the margins Gordons had even worked out weight specifications, gear ratios, and other technical details that would have been absurd if they didn't look so damned plausible.

"You really are an android," said Larry Lepper wonderingly.

"If you had known me before today, you would not have doubted me," said Mr. Gordons. "I do not lie."

"That means you can really turn into other stuff, like the Robokids do. Really?"

"Really. Would you like me to demonstrate?"

"No! I mean, yeah. Maybe." Larry Lepper was thinking at a furious pace. This nut or machine or whatever it was seemed to like him.

"Please make up your mind. I have enemies and now that I understand I cannot rely on the fictitious Commander Robot, I must discover a new form to take so that my enemies will not find me."

"You can turn into anything?"

"Yes. I require only appropriate raw materials to assimilate."

Larry Lepper looked at Mr. Gordons and his all-purpose drawing hand.

"I'm your friend, right?"

"You are my friend, right."

"And you can turn into anything?"

"I have already said that."

"Anything I ask, right?"

"Yes."

"If I asked you to turn into something very, very big, what would you say?"

"I would say what very, very big thing do you want me to assimilate, friend?"

"I'll get my car," said Larry Lepper, deciding that here was one robot he could learn to love, "and show you."

17

At Los Angeles International Airport, the Master of Sinanju rented a car with the privileged air of a diplomat being whisked through customs.

"I'm driving," Remo insisted, as the counter clerk finished processing Chiun's credit card.

"No," said the Master of Sinanju firmly. "I am."

"Little Father, you don't know the roads out here. I do. We'll get there faster if I drive."

"But you do not know our destination," Chiun said triumphantly. "I do."

They walked to the lot in silence. Since Chiun had told Remo that he knew where to find Mr. Gordons, he had refused to say any more. He had asked Harold Smith to book a flight for Los Angeles and went off to change his clothes. Remo was surprised when he returned, not in a gaudy American suit, but wearing a brocaded kimono that Remo estimated weighed close to twenty pounds. The Master of Sinanju had explained that the matter between Sinanju and Gordons was a matter of honor and required ceremonial attire, and that he was not renouncing American dress, despite what Remo might think. He had also suggested that Remo dress more appropriately. Remo had changed his socks.

When they neared the rental car, Remo darted ahead and slipped behind the wheel. He grabbed it in both hands and clung for dear life.

"You are not driving," said the Master of Sinanju testily. "I am. I purchased the use of this conveyance with my wondrous card and I insist upon driving."

"It's a credit card and everyone has one," cried Remo.

"Not like mine. Mine is gold, and merchants do not burden me with requests for money when I use it."

Remo, who had tried repeatedly to explain how credit cards really worked, and failed, sighed and said, "I'm driving. Just tell me where I'm going."

The Master of Sinanju stamped a sandaled foot. "If you do not step out this instant I will have you arrested." He made a show of looking around for a policeman.

"Tell you what, Little Father," Remo said lightly. "Let me drive down so you get to know the roads and I'll let you drive us back. Fair enough?"

"I wish to drive both ways," Chiun said stubbornly. "Sometimes the roads are not the same in both directions."

"Look, if I drive, you can concentrate on navigation. Anna told me you were a wonderful driver, but needed more navigation practice."

"She said that?" asked Chiun.

"Absolutely," lied Remo.

"I take back every bad thing I said about her," said Chiun, stepping around to the passenger side.

"Where to?" asked Remo when Chiun settled into the passenger side.

"I will not tell you. I wish it to be a surprise."

"Then how am I going to get there?"

"Give me a map and I will inform you of each step."

"Oh, for crying out loud," Remo sighed, reaching into the glove compartment and pulling out a folded road map. "Here."

The Master of Sinanju delicately unfolded the map and studied it for some moments, tracing several routes with a long-nailed finger. Remo tried to peer over the

edge of the map, and Chiun shifted in his seat so that
his back was to Remo.

Remo folded his arms and looked bored.

Finally Chiun said, "Leave this parking area."

Remo sent the car out of the lot and asked, "Now
what?"

"Left."

"This will go a lot smoother if I'm not working from
connect-the-dots directions," Remo complained. "Could
you possibly see fit to give a town to aim for? Please."

"Very well," said Chiun petulantly. "We are going
first to Inglewood."

Remo fought the traffic along Manchester Boulevard
until they hit Inglewood, and asked, "Now?"

"Follow this same road south."

Remo drove until the road took him to Firestone
Boulevard and finally linked up with the Santa Ana
Freeway. It was only ten in the morning and traffic was
just a step away from being gridlocked.

"I do not know why you did not wish me to drive,"
said Chiun, his eyes peeled for cars decorated with
fuzzy dice. "We are spending most of our time standing
still."

Because he was in no mood for an argument, Remo
asked about something that had been bothering him.
"When Smith gave that credit card to you, what exactly
did he say?"

"He said I was responsible for it."

"Responsible. That was the word he used?"

"Exactly. Why do you ask?"

"Oh, nothing," said Remo. "By the way, have you
been getting a lot of strange mail lately?"

"Some. All junk. I throw it out unread."

"I see," said Remo.

"Why did you ask that question?" Chiun wanted to
know.

"Oh, no reason. Just to kill time."

The traffic got worse the further south they traveled. When they entered the town limits of Anaheim, it was almost at a standstill.

"This next exit," said Chiun at the last possible minute.

Remo sent the car sliding off the ramp with a screech of tires. "A little more warning next time, huh?" he said.

"We are almost there."

"Where?" But Remo knew where almost as soon as the words were out of his mouth. He braked the car.

"Oh, no," he said, looking at the huge sign gracing the entrance to a sprawling parking area: DISNEYLAND.

"Oh, yes," said the Master of Sinanju proudly.

Grimly Remo drove into the lot and parked the car. With Chiun trailing behind him, he strode to the row of ticket booths. A digital sign for keeping track of admissions stood off to one side. The current number was 257,998,677.

Remo groaned.

"Do you not agree with me that this is where Gordons has come?" Chiun said.

"Yeah, Little Father, I do," Remo said hoarsely. He was thinking of the numbers of people who passed through the gates of Disneyland every day. He could remember reading that more than three million people had visited Disneyland since opening day. That meant thousands each year. And every one of them potential victims of Mr. Gordons' microwave sterilization plan.

Remo walked up to one of the booths. The ticket girl practically hugged him.

"Oh goody, a customer!" she squealed delightedly.

"Why the surprise?" asked Remo. "Don't you get hundreds of people here every day?"

"Look around. Do you see any hundreds of people?"

Remo looked around. There were only the other

ticket takers, looking at Remo with longing expressions.
He looked back at the parking area. Except for Remo's
car, it, too, was empty. In the background the famous
Disneyland monorail scooted along its raised track, every car vacant.

"Where are all the people?" Remo asked.

"We haven't had any ever since that other place
opened up," the ticket girl confided.

"What other place?" asked Remo.

"Don't tell him," the other ticket takers hissed.

"Too late," said Remo. "Tell me."

"Larryland. It's down in Santa Ana. It sprang up
practically overnight, and ever since it did, people have
been going there instead of here."

"So what? They'll come back when the novelty wears
off."

"Not this novelty. Larryland gives free admission."

"Did you say free?" asked Chiun, who had been
looking in vain for Mickey Mouse.

"Yeah. And it's twice the size of this place. That will
be thirteen dollars for two adult admissions, please,"
she added.

Remo ignored her and turned to Chiun.

"Little Father, I think you were wrong."

"But not far wrong," Chiun insisted. "I think we
should venture to this upstart Larryland. After we have
visited Frontierland, that is. I have always wanted to
see Frontierland."

"Frontierland was dismantled years ago, Little Father," Remo said gently.

Chiun sucked in his cheeks with disappointment.
"No!" he gasped.

"I'm afraid so."

Chiun brushed past Remo and accosted the ticket
girl.

"Frontierland. It is no more?"

"Long gone," said the girl.

"Do you have any more of the fur caps with the long tails?"

"Davy Crockett hats are collector's items now. You can't get them anymore."

Chiun turned on Remo. "You should have brought me here sooner," he said, and stormed off to the car.

"This was your idea, remember?" Remo shouted. Then he ran after the Master of Sinanju in case Chiun decided that his only solace after this grievous disappointment would be to get behind the wheel of an automobile.

"Does this mean you're not coming in after all?" the ticket girl called after them.

Colonel Rshat Kirlov had always dreamed of one day visiting the United States of America. He never imagined he would cross the border walking on his hands and knees, leading soldiers who crawled like dogs.

At thirty-seven years of age, Colonel Kirlov was a squat bull of a man whose swarthy skin betrayed a hint of Tatar blood. His black hair was as coarse as horsehair. He would never pass for an American, but he could pass for a Mexican peasant, which was why he had been selected for this mission.

Mexicans would not mistake him for one of their own, however. That was why Colonel Rshat Kirlov kept his distance from the occasional real migrant worker as he led ten handpicked soldiers, mostly enlistees from the Asiatic republics of Uzbekistan and Tashkent, across the desert on their hands and knees. They were dressed in the Mexican peasant clothes which had been provided to them at the embassy in Mexico City, where they had been flown directly from Moscow. They had donned the garments when they got to the dusty bor-

der town of Sonoita, to which they had been driven in a
rickety bus.

There they had set out on foot for the Arizona border.

The embassy had briefed him that the border was not
heavily patrolled. Although the American government
frowned upon the migrant workers who stole up from
Mexico, they also needed them to harvest their fruit
crops. Crossing would be comparatively easy, he was
assured.

Colonel Kirlov was not a man to take chances. So he
had his men drop to their knees and, leading the way,
he showed them how to walk on their knees and just
the tips of their fingers. The tracks they left would look
uncannily like those of a hopping jackrabbit. That was
to fool the American border police.

They traveled for three miles in this fashion, with hot
desert sand burning their fingertips and windblown
sand abrading their faces. Colonel Rshat Kirlov worried
that their fingers would be too raw to pull gun triggers
when the time came, but inasmuch as he had been
forbidden to carry weapons into the United States, it
did not seem especially important just then.

When Colonel Kirlov finally gave the order to stand,
they were on American soil.

They ambushed a camper van on a lonely road. Kirlov
waved his cotton shirt in the face of the oncoming
vehicle, and when it slowed, his men leapt from out of
the rocks. That they were unarmed made no difference.
There was only a middle-aged man and his wife and
their dog. They killed all three with bare hands, bury-
ing all but the dog by the side of the road. They buried
the dog too, but only after they had eaten the meat.

Colonel Kirlov's orders were to reach the town of
Vaya Chin, near the Papago Indian Reservation, and
wait.

When Anna Chutesov showed up two days later, she

took one look at the hijacked camper and said, "Good. You are not as big a fool as I would have expected. We will need this."

Colonel Rshat Kirlov was not used to having a woman talk to him like that. Especially one who was not a KGB officer. He started to raise his voice in protest.

Anna Chutesov slapped him in the face. It was the shock more than the pain that stilled his tongue.

Disdainfully the blond woman turned her back on him and addressed his men, who were lined up at attention. "I have brought you all American tourist clothes," she said, tossing bundled packages at their feet. "Go behind those rocks and change while I load your equipment on the vehicle."

When Colonel Kirlov opened his package, he discovered a gaudy Hawaiian shirt and Bermuda shorts. Changing clothes in silence, he felt like a fool. Looking at his men climbing into their new clothes, he knew he looked like one too.

Kirlov sat in the back of the camper during the drive across the desert to the place that Anna Chutesov, breaking a long smoldering silence, told them was California. She kept adjusting a beeping device that sat in her lap. Often she raised it, turning a loop antenna this way or that, and sending the camper in confused circles. Kirlov knew she was homing in on some radio signal. But that was all he knew.

Finally, after many long hours in which the driven blond woman had refused to give any of them a turn at the wheel, they stopped on a great black highway where the traffic was backed up until they could drive no further.

Anna Chutesov stood up.

"We can go no further. The rest of the way we will travel on foot. In twos. You will find your weapons in the overhead compartments."

The men fell on the compartments like thirsty dogs. They had been alone in an enemy land too long without weapons. Weapons would make them feel like men again.

Colonel Kirlov pulled out a stubby Uzi with a folding stock and looked at his men. They, too, had brought forth identical weapons.

"No Kalashnikov rifles?" Kirlov said to no one in particular.

"The Uzi is an excellent field weapon and easily concealed," said Anna Chutesov. "Gather up extra ammunition clips and form your men into pairs. I will direct them on when to exit."

"Where are we going?"

Anna Chutesov pointed out of the windshield, beyond the lines of honking, smoking cars.

Colonel Rshat Kirlov squinted. Not many hundreds of yards away was a great encampment. Towers climbed to the sky. A peculiar wheel turned against the sun, like a cog in a great machine. Flying machines darted like dragonflies.

Colonel Rshat Kirlov nodded. Obviously the place was an important American installation. Probably a space complex, for Kirlov knew of the recent loss of the *Yuri Gagarin*.

He tried to read the enormous sign over the entrance, but he could translate only the last part of the complex's official title.

He turned to one of his men, whose English was better than his own.

"What means 'Larry'?" he asked.

"I do not know the word."

"We are obviously going to that secret American space complex ahead," he whispered to the others. "Do any of you know what that word on the great sign means?"

The men took turns squinting at the large sign.

But none of them could translate the peculiar name Larryland into proper Russian. And the cold Anna Chutesov refused to enlighten them.

18

Larry Lepper was lord and master of all he surveyed.

Standing on the top of a fairyland minaret, he enjoyed the spectacular panorama that was Larryland. From the main gate, where the crowds streamed in through the opening in the shape of Buster Bear's smiling mouth, to the hundred-foot statues of Squirrel Girl, Magic Mouse, and other Larry Lepper creations, he owned it all. Children played in the plastic-cobbled streets. Their shrieks of joy radiated from the Room of the Creepers, laughter welled up from the Hologram House, and the smells of popcorn, cotton candy, and fried dough wafted into the dry heat of the southern California afternoon.

Larry had it all. No more slaving away at a drawing board. Never again would he have to work for the likes of Bill Banana or draw another robot. In fact, producers were banging at the door to option his characters. Larry had always assumed that he would achieve his dream the other way around—get the characters on the air first and hope they led to a theme park. But it had come true the easy way.

And best of all, it had happened overnight.

Larry had led the strange Mr. Gordons to the site, a deserted theme park that had gone bankrupt trying to compete with Disneyland.

"Can you do something with this?" Larry had asked.

It was night. Mr. Gordons simply walked through the chain-link fence, cutting a hole large enough to pass through with fingers like wire cutters. He walked over to the deserted Ferris wheel and into the control booth. Not through the door, but literally into the wall. Larry had blinked, and the wall had seemed to absorb Gordons.

Larry had felt a trembling in the ground, and suddenly, like the color filling the screen in *The Wizard of Oz*, the park came to life. Larry rushed in like a child.

He had spent the first evening overseeing adjustments. He had only to ask the Ferris wheel to change and it became the Squirrel Girl ride, complete with colorful images of Squirrel Girl on each hub.

When the last attraction, the sprawling Moon Walk, had been modified, Larry was satisfied.

"We'll make millions," he cried. "What should I charge for admission?"

"Nothing," said the voice of Mr. Gordons, which this time came from the Moon Walk entrance, which Gordons had designed so that no one could leave the park without enjoying it.

"Nothing? How will I make money?"

"You will make money on the concessions," said Mr. Gordons. "But it is important that large numbers of people pass through Larryland."

"Larryland? I was going to call it Lepperland."

"Lepperland has an unfortunate connotation," pointed out Mr. Gordons, whose voice now crackled from the Buster Bear statue as Larry made his rounds. Larry quickly got used to the voice coming from different places. He had worked in a fantasy world so long that nothing surprised him. Not even the fact that the entire park was a thinking android.

"I had my heart set on Lepperland," he complained.

"Names are important. I learned this in my last occupation."

"What was that?" Larry asked, curious.

"I was a car wash."

"You mean, you worked in a car wash."

"No," said Mr. Gordons. "I *was* the car wash."

"Oh."

And because Mr. Gordons had provided Larry Lepper with his dream, Larry had not complained or objected. He had rushed out to place ads in the newspapers so that when the first rush of families came, he was all set to greet them in his Buster Bear suit.

That had been just one hectic day before. Now Larry was taking a break from being Buster Bear and enjoying the view from his private tower.

"Ah, what could possibly go wrong now?" Larry said aloud.

The voice of Mr. Gordons came from the air-conditioning vent. "There is trouble in Larryland, Larry Lepper," it said.

"What trouble?" Larry asked, bringing his face close to the vent.

"Several men are coming in through the entrance, carrying automatic weapons."

Larry looked down. Lines of cars stretched out from the parking lot like beetles on a conveyor belt. Cars honked impatiently. And across the tops of a string of vehicles stomped several men in gaudy tourist clothes.

They pushed their way through the crowd. They carried beach towels and Larry didn't have to guess as to what the towels concealed. He knew from the two-handed way the towels were carried, one hand under and the other on top, holding the towels in place.

"What do I do?" demanded Larry Lepper.

"Find out what they want. It is imperative that there be no disruption in the functioning of this theme park."

"My thinking exactly," said Larry Lepper resolutely.

Larry Lepper donned his oversize Buster Bear head and waddled down the winding steps, his heart in his mouth. He wondered if the Mafia had come to demand a piece of the Larryland action.

Anna Chutesov was surrounded.

She stood in a sea of children, trying to isolate the radio transmission. It was important that she stay in one place long enough to get one leg of the signal. The children milled around her and it only made her acutely aware of the horror that was masked under the harlequin name of Larryland. How many of them, she wondered, would never develop into puberty because of this innocent day in the sun?

When a little girl skipped by, bumping Anna's head with a Buster Bear balloon, Anna turned on her with the fury born of frustration.

"Go away!" she hissed. "Can you not see that I am doing something important?"

The little girl stopped, looked stunned, and rushed off crying, "Mommy, Mommy."

Anna Chutesov returned to her radio locator, biting her lip. Every moment she was delayed finding the Sword of Damocles, more parents, more children, would be exposed to its microwaves. Somewhere, Anna knew, the satellite was doing its insidious work. But where? Which of these rides was stripping those who walked through it of the ability to bear children?

Anna got her first fix, and locking it into the optical viewer, started for the other end of the park.

She didn't get there. She dropped the locator, breaking it. She was looking at the object of her search.

It was a great palace of crystal and chrome. The neon sign in front said MOON WALK. It was the largest building in the park and set near the back. It had the biggest lines, which snaked around a series of posts and lines designed to keep the crowds in place. It was also the only exit from Larryland.

"How diabolical," Anna Chutesov said, hush-voiced. "In order for the people to leave, they must go through the Moon Walk. It is there that I will find what I seek."

Anna found Rshat Kirlov at an ice-cream stand trying to balance a double-scooped pistachio-nut cone.

"Fool," she said, knocking the cone from his hand.

"I was hungry," Colonel Rshat Kirlov whined.

"Never mind. I think I have found the object of my search."

"I will have my men assemble for the assault."

"Let us pray such a moronic measure will be unnecessary," Anna said. "Deploy your men around the attraction called the Moon Walk. Do not—repeat, do not—let them enter. I am going inside. Alone. If I do not return at the end of twenty minutes, you will send in your two best men. Tell them they are to look for what appears to be a satellite. They are not to be fooled by appearances of frivolity. If they see such an object, they are to destroy it at all costs. If the first pair do not return, send in the next, and so on until success."

"I understand."

"No, you do not. You are taking orders and you are obeying them. Understanding is not your function."

"What happens, Comrade Chutesov, if none of my men return from this place?"

"You will go to the Soviet consulate in the city of Los Angeles. It is the large city to the north. Tell them that the Sword is inside that building."

"The sword?"

"The Sword," repeated Anna Chutesov. "Now, instruct your men. The twenty minutes begin when you see me walk through the entrance to the Moon Walk attraction."

Anna Chutesov did not get into the long line leading to the Moon Walk. There was no time. Every delay would sterilize that many more people walking through the building. She struggled through the crowd and hopped a low concrete obstruction until she was near the head of the line. She stepped ahead of the first in line, a family of four. She wanted to warn them, but who would believe her?

Anna did not argue with the teenage boy who controlled the doors. She smiled glassily, and while the boy sputtered something about not breaking in line, Anna led him around to the side wall and squeezed his neck until he lay dead. She wished she did not have to kill him, but it was his life against that of thousands of unborn generations. Without an operator, no one could enter the Moon Walk until Anna Chutesov had neutralized its evil function.

"I smell Russians," said the Master of Sinanju.

Remo Williams paused. They had just made their way past the Buster Bear entrance gate. The crowds seemed too packed to allow passage, but Chiun told Remo to follow his lead.

The crowd probably never understood why they parted before the tiny Oriental in the white brocade kimono. Some felt an itch and moved aside to scratch it. Others felt pressure against their backs, but when they looked back, they saw nothing.

Thus it had gone until Remo had discovered himself deep within the gaiety of Larryland.

He sniffed the air. "Yeah. I smell them too," he said. Long ago. The Master of Sinanju had taught him that all people gave off distinctive odors, a mixture of body chemistry and diet. Although all these personal odors were unique, they could be categorized according to dietary influences. There was the distinctive curry-spice aroma of the East Indian, the hamburger smell of the American, and so on. Russians usually smelled of black bread and potato soup.

"There," said Chiun, pointing.

Remo saw two men in Hawaiian shirts standing about uncomfortably, towels held at hip level.

"Think they have guns?" Remo asked.

"They will need them. They reek of suspicion."

"Anna must have beat us to the punch, Little Father."

"Perhaps," said the Master of Sinanju distantly. He was not watching the Russians. He was scanning the park, looking for the most probable hiding place of the Sword of Damocles. He dismissed the tallest structure—a large tower—because he sensed no energy emanating from it. The Squirrel Girl wheel was too open. There was no place amid its skeletal works to conceal a spherical object. That left the walk-in attractions.

"I don't see Anna, but I count ten Russians, all armed, hanging around the Moon Walk," Remo said. "What do you suppose that means?"

The Master of Sinanju turned his attention on the Moon Walk. The attraction had the longest line, meaning that it was the most popular. It was also surrounded, as Remo had pointed out, by Russian agents.

Chiun faced Remo and looked him in the eye.

"Listen to me, Remo, for this is important," he said.

"I'm listening," said Remo, watching the Russians out of the corner of his eye.

"Then listen with your eyes too," snapped Chiun, clapping his hands so sharply that nearby pigeons took wing.

"Okay, okay."

"I have lost something important to me," Chiun scolded. "I will not lose you too."

"I can handle whatever comes," Remo said.

"Nor will I countenance your losing your seed. Someday you will have need of it, when the time comes to train the next Master after you. Look around you, Remo.

Look at these people. Look at the husbands and wives
and the precious little children."

Remo looked. Everywhere, he saw joy. A father picked
up a small boy so he could better see a greeter dressed
as Magic Mouse juggling white balls. Twin brothers
took turns eating from the same cotton-candy cone,
their mouths pink and sticky. It made Remo wish he
was a child all over again.

"What do you see?" asked Chiun.

"I see a lot of people having fun. Makes me wish I
was one of them."

"I see children who will never know the joy of a new
sibling coming into their lives," intoned the Master of
Sinanju. "I see parents who have created life for the
final time and do not realize it. I see women who will
never enjoy the miracle and wonder of birth. I see
fathers who will never again behold their likeness in a
baby's face. I see a desert of suffering. Meditate upon
that, Remo, my son, and tell me again what you see
about you."

Remo looked again.

"I see horror," he said.

"Good, for now you see true. Some of these people
may be saved from such a destiny, but you must obey
my every command, for there is little time."

"Say the word, Little Father," Remo said resolutely.
"I'll do whatever you ask."

The Master of Sinanju nodded. "The Russians look
nervous," he said. "They have many guns and there are
many innocents about. You will attend to them. Use all
your skill, for no bullets must fly."

"They've seen their last sunset. What about you?"

"I will search for the instrument of infertility, and
Gordons. Do not follow me, for you must not risk your
seed too. That is the most important part."

"I can't let you go up against Gordons alone," Remo protested.

"And I cannot let you become an empty vessel," Chiun retorted. "If you will not do this for me, or for Sinanju, then think of your betrothed, who awaits your return."

"Mah-Li," said Remo.

"Yes, Mah-Li may wish to bear your children, although why is beyond me. Keep Mah-Li in mind, lest you do something foolish. Now attend to the Russians while I search these buildings, beginning with this one. Whatever you do, whatever happens, do not follow me into any of them until I have destroyed the round sword of the Russians."

"Gotcha, Little Father," Remo promised.

And the Master of Sinanju melted into the crowd. Remo tried to follow him with his eyes, but it was impossible to spot his tiny figure moving through the masses of tall American tourists.

Colonel Rshat Kirlov understood his orders. He was to await the return of Anna Chutesov or the passing of twenty minutes. In the meantime, he was to do nothing. While he waited, he wondered why as bold a stroke as the infiltration of America by a crack KGB team would lead to a place such as Larryland. He understood that Larryland was a place like the famous Disneyland, about which he had read. Everyone knew about Disneyland, even in Soviet Russia.

Vaguely he wondered if Anna Chutesov's mission was to steal American theme-park technology. Perhaps there would soon be such places all over Mother Russia. He wondered if they would be called something like Leninland.

A seven-foot polyester bear interrupted his thoughts.

"Excuse me," said the bear. "But I must ask you to

check your guns at the gate. I'm sure they're not real, but even water pistols are not permitted here. We have a strict no-weapons policy. It's for everybody's safety, naturally."

"Go away," said Rshat Kirlov. "I know nothing of what you are speaking to me about."

"Look, I don't want to have to call the police."

"And I do not want you to call the police," said Colonel Rshat Kirlov, pressing the concealed muzzle of his Uzi machine pistol into the bear's fat paunch.

When Remo Williams gave up looking for the Master of Sinanju, he saw that three of the Russians had surrounded one of the official Larryland greeters, someone in a big bear suit. The trio pressed colorful beach towels against the bear suit, and were forcing the man inside to walk behind the big Moon Walk pavilion.

"Excuse me," Remo said, barging in on them. "But that's a national treasure you're assaulting."

"National—?" began Colonel Rshat Kirlov.

"Absolutely," said Remo. "Don't you recognize Yogi Bear when you see him?"

"Buster," corrected Larry Lepper, inside the suit. "Buster Bear."

"Shut up," said Remo. "Now, as I was saying, this man is a big American media star, and a close personal friend of Smokey the Bear. Why don't you leave him alone?"

"What do you not mind your own business?"

"Okay," said Remo airily. "I asked nice. Didn't you people hear me ask nice?"

"Yes," said Larry Lepper nervously. "I did."

Remo decided that the Russians weren't the problem. Their weapons were. He took the weapons of the two nearest men away from them with a one-handed sweep. The third man, the one who had been speaking and the apparent leader, saw Remo hold up two Uzis in one hand and the covering towels in the other. He hesitated.

The hesitation was momentary. Remo's kick was lightning.

Colonel Rshat Kirlov felt his Uzi leap into the air. Remo caught it coming down. The towel fluttered after it, and Remo got it too.

"Now, watch carefully," Remo said. The Russians watched. So did Lepper, peering through the eyeholes concealed in Buster Bear's smiling mouth.

Remo tucked one of the Uzis under an arm and, with a steel-hard forefinger, proceeded to stuff a beach towel down the weapon's blunt muzzle like a magician loading colored scarves into a hollow wand. He tossed the weapon back at its owner and performed the same operation on the other two machine pistols before returning them.

"Ta-dah," he sang. "Nothing up my sleeves, either."

"What means 'ta-dah'?" asked Colonel Rshat Kirlov, looking at the weapon in his hand. He stared down the muzzle. It was dark. There was obviously no beach towel inside, although to the naked eye it had looked as though the crazy American had stuffed the thick towel into the gun. Colonel Kirlov knew that could not be. The muzzle of an Uzi would barely accommodate a pencil, never mind a very thick towel.

"Are your weapons clear?" he asked the other men.

The nodded.

"Then use them."

Remo stood with his arms folded while three trigger fingers depressed three triggers and three hands shattered into raw bone and blood. The men did not have time to scream. They never realized that their guns had backfired and exploded. Remo danced up to each of them and took them out with stiff-fingered strokes to their frontal lobes.

"What happened?" asked Larry Lepper dully. The three men lay on the ground.

"They died," Remo said unconcernedly. He was looking for more Russians. He saw two more, standing like Hawaiian versions of Mafia bodyguards before the Moon Walk pavilion. "Excuse me while I go kill some more."

"Nice meeting you," said Larry Lepper, grateful that he would not have to deal with the armed men.

"Give Smokey my best," Remo called back.

The sound of the exploding Uzis had gone unnoticed in the carnival sounds of Larryland, so the next pair of Russians had no idea that there had been trouble. They stood at attention, oblivious of the crowds swirling around them.

Remo slipped up from behind and took an elbow in each hand. The men felt a sudden irresistible urge to drop their weapons. They did.

Remo scooped up the Uzis and removed the clips. "There," he said. "Now that they're empty, I've got some questions for the two of you." He pointed the weapons at them.

"Excuse me," said one of the Russians. "But you are mistaken."

"I am?" asked Remo. He frowned.

"Yes. Those weapons are not empty."

"Nonsense," Remo said. "You saw me take out the clips."

"There is always a round in the chamber. Be so good as to remove those before you wave them like that."

"I think you're thinking of some other weapon," Remo said.

"I am sure I am correct," the Russian said with studied politeness. "I am a soldier."

"Really?" said Remo. And because he resented the

presence of Soviet soldiers in an American theme park, he did something he had not done since learning Sinanju. He pressed the trigger.

The complaining Russian folded like a broken board.

"What do you know?" Remo said. "He was right, after all. I guess that means there's another round in this gun too." He pointed it at the second Russian's face.

"What do you wish to know?" the Russian asked unhappily.

"For starters, I'd like to know where Anna Chutesov is."

The Russian jerked a thumb at the Moon Walk pavilion, which glittered directly behind him.

"She is there, looking for something. We know not what."

"You just answered my second question," Remo said.

"Is that good?"

"For me, yes. For you, uh-uh," Remo told him, shaking his head sadly.

"You are going to shoot me here?"

"No, I hate guns. Firing that one made me remember why. It's noisy and sloppy, and why should I shoot you when I can do this?" And Remo flipped the gun at the Russian. It struck him square over the heart, stopping it.

"Much better," Remo said, looking around for more Russians.

The Master of Sinanju found himself walking through a long, square tunnel whose walls might have been carved from black obsidian. Starlike lights twinkled behind the smoky glass, giving the illusion of walking through a tunnel of stars. When he emerged at last, he found himself in a spherical white room.

The room was turning like the inside of a basketball

rolling down a hill. It was filled with children and adults, laughing and giggling as they tumbled about the slick inner walls.

When the room stopped revolving, an opening appeared on the opposite side, leading deeper into the Moon Walk attraction. The children started for the opening first.

The Master of Sinanju cleared space in a gazellelike leap. He landed, blocking the entrance, his spindly arms raised menacingly.

"Begone!" he said wrathfully.

The children giggled, thinking the Master of Sinanju was part of the attraction.

"Are you a moon man?" one of them asked.

"This place is closed. Begone," Chiun repeated. And when one of the children reached out to touch the brocade of his robe, he slapped him once. Not hard, but sharply enough to get the attention of the others.

"How dare you strike my child!" a woman cried, shoving her way toward the Master of Sinanju. Chiun smacked her too, and spinning her around, sent her off with a firm sandal on the seat of her pants.

"I have closed this place," he said loudly. "Go now, and tell the others that no one may enter henceforth, otherwise they will face the wrath of the Master of Sinanju."

"And you'll face the wrath of my lawyer," the woman shot back. But she led the crying child back toward the entrance. The others followed.

Satisfied that he had prevented a terrible fate from befalling the group, the Master of Sinanju turned to face the next room and pressed on. His face was set.

Anna Chutesov felt the eyes upon her.

She had walked through the Star Tunnel and the Satellite Spin and floated through the Orbit Room to

find herself in a great room called the Sargasso of Lost
Spaceships. The floor was a web of nylon mesh. Great
rusty hulks of derelict spaceships lay all about her.
They protruded up from the bouncing mesh flooring,
stuck out of the walls, and floated under the ceiling.
She brushed at a tiny asteroid that hung before her
face, but her hand went through it. She realized it was
a three-dimensional image.

The room was burnished with an eerie blue glow. In
the semilit portholes of the spaceships, there were dum-
mies of astronauts and aliens, supposedly dead and
marooned in space. Their eyes stared, open and seem-
ingly alive.

Anna walked past a dummy in an astronaut suit,
picking her way carefully because the web flooring gave
with each step like a trampoline, making it seem as if
she were actually walking in space. She thought she
heard the crinkling sound of a spacesuit flexing.

Anna stopped to listen, but the floor continued to
shake.

Anna Chutesov wheeled suddenly, her pistol coming
up.

The dummy in the spacesuit clambered to its feet
and faced her. Its unblinking blue eyes regarded her
blankly.

"Hello is all right," said the voice. The same voice
that had called to her from the booth of the Yuri Gagarin Free Car Wash.

"I prefer good-bye," spat Anna Chutesov, and she
emptied the clip into the figure's chest.

19

Remo Williams had lost count.

There had been ten Russians altogether. He was pretty sure of that number. He had counted them before he had gone to work on them. The trouble was, he had not bothered to count them as he dispatched them.

Remo thought he had gotten all ten. But he wasn't sure. He sat down on a grassy knoll where the legend "Larryland" was spelled out in daisies and cornflowers, and counted them off on his fingers. There had been the first three, whose guns exploded. Then the next two, one of whom he had shot. A bad move. He would never do that again. Remo recalled stuffing one Russian into a trash receptacle. That made five so far. Then there had been the one who had picked up a little boy and tried to use him as a shield when Remo had cornered him. Remo had rescued the boy and fed the Russian to the big gears of the Squirrel Girl ride. That had been a mistake too, because the man had screamed in Russian as the machinery ground up his legs. And that had brought the others running.

That was where it turned complicated.

Did three Russians try to jump him—or was it four? If Remo could remember for certain, it might account for all of them.

Remo had had to run into the crowd, and the Russians followed him, so Remo had to play it carefully. He sneaked up on the first one, crouching low, working the crowd so that the first target noticed nothing. The other Russians saw their comrade suddenly drop from sight. Remo had pulled him to the ground and collapsed his windpipe.

The second Russian disappeared beneath a sea of people in exactly the same way, and Remo, because it had seemed fitting, had made the "duh-duh-duh-duh-duh-duh" sound that was the theme from *Jaws* as he bore down, unseen, on the third and possibly last guard.

Remo tapped that man's spine, and carried him off to the pile he had made of the others, out of sight behind a cluster of palms.

So was it three or four? Remo couldn't remember. He thought it was four, but he wasn't positive. He wished he had counted. Probably it was four, because he didn't find any more Russians. Maybe the last one had run away.

While he was trying to figure it out, the man in the Buster Bear suit came up to him.

"I think someone's calling you," he said helpfully.

"Where?" Remo asked, coming to his feet. "Where?"

"There," said the bear, pointing.

Remo followed the bear's pointing paw. In a side door to the Moon Walk pavilion, the face of Anna Chutesov had appeared.

"Remo," her urgent voice called out. "Hurry. Chiun needs you."

Remo hesitated only a moment. Chiun had told him to stay outside. But now he was sending the message that he needed help. That decided Remo. He flashed to the door.

Anna Chutesov had already disappeared inside. Remo spotted her at the end of a dim passageway. She looked back and waved him on.

Remo followed, noticing that on either side of the

passage, a copper line, like a transistor radio circuit, ran the length of both walls. He wondered why it would be exposed like that, then saw that Anna brushed either line casually as she walked, and he knew the wires must be safe.

"Wait up," he called after her.

"There is no time," she called back. "Hurry."

Remo followed her into a room that was completely dark. His eyes adjusted instantly. He saw Anna Chutesov's dim figure disappear through a door.

Remo stepped through. The next room was full of mellow golden light.

Anna Chutesov stood off to one side. She stood with her fingertips touching the continuous copper line, and Remo noticed that the tips of her fingers, like the wire, were coppery.

"Hello is all right," Anna Chutesov said in the voice of Mr. Gordons.

"You never did learn to talk right, tin man," Remo said. And because he knew that the real Anna Chutesov had to be dead, he started in on Gordons without wasting another moment.

The voice of the Master of Sinanju stopped him.

"Remo!" Chiun called. "Go back! Do you hear me? Go back."

Remo, distracted, turned to the sound of his voice.

He saw a panorama of a lunar landscape, artificial rock and craters dotting the floor. From the ground, stalagmites rose like spiny needles, and over his head stars twinkled against a glassy black sky and planets loomed gigantically.

In the middle of the ceiling hung the planet Saturn, a silvery ball crowned by a yellow ring.

And immediately below Saturn, clinging to a needle of stone and clawing like a cat for the ringed planet, was the Master of Sinanju.

"Chiun! You okay?" Remo called.

"I hear disappointment shouting in a loud voice, asking me if I am okay," Chiun said angrily. "I am not okay. I am risking my life to protect an idiot. Go! Save your seed."

Before Remo could answer, his vision exploded in a starburst of pain.

Gordons had struck the first blow.

Remo stepped back, weaved to avoid a second, killing blow, and steeled himself. He knew he was facing Mr. Gordons, his old enemy. But Mr. Gordons looked exactly like Anna Chutesov. That would make it harder.

"Remo. Go this instant!" Chiun cried, his cheeks puffing out with rage. "I will handle this."

"After I settle this little score," Remo said. He lunged for Gordons' chest. The blow sent sparks flying, but Mr. Gordons remained on his feet. The android clutched at the wall for support, feeling the copper wire, then came on.

Remo knew from past experience that the element containing Gordons' intelligence, the nearly indestructible control circuits, were not always located in the same part of his mechanical body. They could be hidden in the android's head, throat, elbow—even in his little finger. Stopping Gordons meant locating and immobilizing that motivating element.

Remo decided not to waste time.

"I'm going to show you a new game," he said. "It's called process of elimination."

He jumped back, bounced off the wall, and kicked against Gordons' chest with both feet. Gordons fell. Remo landed on top of him. He took off the android's right arm with a vicious chop. Gordons, squealing like a tape recorder, swept Remo aside with the other arm.

"Nope, it's not in that arm," Remo said, getting back his legs.

"Remo! Go!" Chiun called in anguish. He was at the tip of the stone needle, within reach of the planet Saturn, which Remo understood was the Sword of Damocles satellite in disguise.

The needle slowly sank into the floor, taking Chiun with it. The Master of Sinanju leapt to another needle as the artificial planet began to revolve in Remo's direction. Its bottom dropped open to reveal its toothlike microwave emitters.

"Remo, it is pointing at you!" Chiun cried. "Run now. We will fight this creature another day."

"Nothing doing," said Remo. "He got Anna. And I'm going to get him."

"I did not want to fight you," Mr. Gordons said. "I would have been content to outlive you, knowing that the House of Sinanju ended with you."

"There isn't room for both of us on this planet," said Remo.

"I will remember your words when I watch the last human being die," said Mr. Gordons, raising his remaining fist.

Remo ducked under Gordons' balled fist, and bobbed up behind him. He batted Gordons' head off. It flew to the other side of the room like a puppet whose string had been jerked.

"Nope. Not in the head either," said Remo.

Mr. Gordons staggered around in circles until he bumped into the wall. He groped for the copper line. When he found it, his jerky movements straightened.

Remo, unaware that the Sword of Damocles' emitters were zeroing in on him, moved in for the kill.

The Master of Sinanju felt his fingernails scratch the Sword of Damocles. The touch was brief. Then, once again, the stalagmite on which he stood retracted into the moonscape floor.

He leapt to the floor, where he swiftly considered the situation. He could rush to Remo's side and pull him from the room and possibly save him from Gordons' mad attack. But that would still leave the hellish device. It would burn the vitality from his pupil's loins before he crossed the room. The Master of Sinanju hesitated.

Then he noticed an object at his feet. It looked like the head of Anna Chutesov, but its neck ended in a cluster of wires and optical fibers.

The Master of Sinanju swept the head up by its blond hair and sent it flying. He had made his decision.

Remo waited for the next blow. When it came, he moved back from it, taking Gordons' remaining wrist in a two-handed grip. He pulled, turning the momentum of the android's thrust against him in a throw that was too perfect to be mere judo. It was Sinanju.

Gordons went flying. His hand came off at the wrist.

Mr. Gordons staggered toward the wall, toward the copper wire that ran around the room.

Remo stepped in ahead of the jerking automaton and yanked a length of the copper filament from the wall, breaking the circuit.

The body of Mr. Gordons collapsed in a heap.

"Yep," Remo said, pleased with himself. "It was in the left hand this time."

"And you are out of your mind," said the Master of Sinanju angrily, joining him.

Remo turned. "I'm sorry I disobeyed your instructions, Little Father. He made himself look like Anna and said you needed me."

"And you believed him!"

"I didn't stop to think. I just knew that you needed me."

"I need an intelligent pupil, that is what I need,"

sputtered the Master of Sinanju. "One who has sense enough to obey the words that come from my lips, not the trickery of an impostor."

"Is that the thanks I get for stopping Gordons?"

"Pah! You did not stop him. I stopped him. Look."

Remo saw that the Sword of Damocles satellite was lying in an artificial crater. It was shattered like a dropped Christmas-tree ornament. The head that resembled Anna Chutesov lay to one side, staring glassily through hair that Remo knew had belonged to the real Anna Chutesov. He turned away from the sight.

"You stopped the satellite," said Remo. "I stopped Gordons."

"When I destroyed the round sword, the machine man collapsed. His thinking parts must have been concealed inside."

"No, it was in his hand," Remo insisted. "He dropped in his tracks when I pulled off the hand."

"No," Chiun said firmly. "I saw him stagger for some moments after that. He sought the copper line, which was the connection to his brain. See? The copper line leads to the ceiling and to the hanging cable."

Remo looked. Sure enough, the filament traced along the ceiling and ran into the suspension cable from which the Sword of Damocles had hung.

"No, no," said Remo. "You don't understand electronics. He probably controlled the satellite through the wire."

"No, the satellite controlled him. That was why he kept touching the wire. Gordons had learned from his past mistakes. He knew that you would seek to destroy him in combat by wrecking his thinking parts. So he sent a false version of himself to do his fighting, operated by removed control."

"Remote control," Remo corrected.

"Then you accept my theory."

Remo threw up his hands. "Does it matter? One of us got him. It's over."

"It does matter," snapped Chiun. "I got him. The glory is mine. And I would appreciate it if you kept your white mouth shut when I report my great victory to the grateful Emperor Smith."

"Whatever you say, Little Father," Remo said wearily.

The Army Corps of Engineers set off the last explosive charge, sending a smoking pile of debris quaking into the air.

"Well, that's the end of Larryland," said Remo.

He watched the mushrooming cloud of dirt and debris slowly lift, pause, then collapse in on itself.

"And of the evil creature Gordons," added the Master of Sinanju. "Thanks to me."

"Are you going to start that again?" sighed Remo.

"Start what?" asked Dr. Harold W. Smith. He had flown in from New York to personally oversee the operation. The Army thought he was a civilian attached to the Environmental Protection Agency.

"Never mind," said Remo. "A family quarrel. It's a shame to destroy Larryland so soon. I never got to go on any of the rides."

"Larryland was Mr. Gordons," said Smith. "He had assimilated the entire park. That's why we're having it pulverized. You'll recall that as long as any functioning piece of Gordons remains intact, he's capable of reconstructing himself."

"Chiun and I smashed every particle of Mr. Gordons' body," Remo assured him.

"No," said the Master of Sinanju stubbornly. "Remo wasted his time dismembering a dummy. I obliterated the round sword of the Russians, which truly contained Gordons' wicked brain."

"In any case," Smith went on, "destroying Larryland should put a period to this whole affair."

"Not to mention making certain that Gordons won't ever come back again," Remo added.

"I think we can be assured of that this time," said Smith, watching the dust settle over Larryland.

"What are you telling the Russians?" Remo asked him.

"Almost nothing. A low-level Soviet delegation is on its way to New York to take possession of the *Yuri Gagarin* and the bodies of its crew. The latter are in sealed caskets, of course."

"I'd love to see the looks on their faces when you present them with the keys to a car wash." Remo chuckled.

Smith ventured a rare smile. "I would too. But I don't think they're going to ask any questions. Not about the Sword of Damocles. They will assume that we have it. That knowledge alone will inhibit them from deploying another."

"What about the guy who owned Larryland?"

"He's undergoing extensive questioning. But I'm satisfied that his story of being a dupe is genuine."

"What will happen to him?"

"No charges will be filed," Smith said. "But I imagine there will be lawsuits once the first symptoms of sterilization show up in the general population. Fortunately, they will be few in number. We've already put out the word that Larryland had to be destroyed because it was built on a toxic-waste site. That should take care of the explanations. What Larry Lepper says in his defense is his problem. But it's doubtful that he will tell the truth. No one would ever believe him."

"Did they find Anna's body?" Remo asked quietly.

"What there was of it that Gordons hadn't assimilated," Smith said grimly. "Along with the KGB team, she will be buried in an anonymous grave. Officially, we don't know what happened to any of them. I doubt that the Soviets will be asking about their whereabouts."

"Anna was a good person."

"She was a valuable ally," Smith admitted. "But she was also a security problem for us. It would have come down to her death sooner or later."

"That's the biz, I guess," Remo said sadly. "I won't forget her soon."

"And I hope that Emperor Smith will not forget that it was his humble servant who finally dispatched Mr. Gordons," Chiun injected. "I would have accomplished this task many years ago, but I was formerly hampered by having to train an unruly pupil at the same time. Now that I am working for the emperor alone, I had no trouble with him."

"I still say the brain was in the hand," Remo mumbled.

"You would," sniffed Chiun.

"All that matters is that Gordons is gone for good," said Smith.

"Amen," added Remo, taking a last look at Larryland.

Epilogue

High over the settling dust that was Larryland, a cracked metallic element reached the apex of its climb. It was beginning the rapid descent to earth when a high wind caught it and sent it tumbling through the clouds. It glittered under the sun, helpless, aimless, and useless.

It would have eventually fallen back to earth to dash itself to pieces on the ground if the jet plane had not come along.

The tiny element was sucked into the port engine.

In the cockpit, the pilot saw the trouble light that warned him the port engine had flamed out.

"Oh, God," he said. Frantically he killed the switch and initiated restarting procedures.

The engine kicked in on the third throw of the switch.

"Whew!" breathed the pilot. "That was almost the last call."

"Definitely," said the co-pilot. "I wouldn't want to make an emergency landing way out here. Not with the Man himself on board."

"Odd, I thought I felt the controls move by themselves," said the pilot.

"Nerves," said the copilot dismissively.

"Probably," agreed the pilot, gripping the controls more tightly. The momentary resistance seemed to go away. Laughing self-consciously, the pilot radioed for landing instructions.

"This is *Air Force One*," he told the tower, "requesting permission to land. Over."

**A riveting thriller of a deadly
and terrifying quest through the streets
of New York—where the toughest knight of all
turns out to be . . . the All-American Girl!**

QUEST

A Novel by
Richard Ben Sapir

Three people are desperately seeking a gold, gem-encrusted saltcellar created for Queen Elizabeth I. But only one of them knows what's really being sought. The Holy Grail is hidden inside and if the others discover the secret, they will have to die!

This suspense-packed search for a priceless gem that is hiding a secret, sweeps you into the intrigue-filled criminal world of international gem dealers—from Cairo to Paris to London to Geneva . . . and holds you breathless to its final page.